A TOR DOUBLE ACTION WESTERN

**Look for Tor Double Action Westerns
from these authors**

MAX BRAND
ZANE GREY
LEWIS B. PATTEN
WAYNE D. OVERHOLSER
CLAY FISHER
FRANK BONHAM
OWEN WISTER
STEVE FRAZEE
HARRY SINCLAIR DRAGO
JOHN PRESCOTT
WILL HENRY*
L. C. TUTTLE*

*coming soon

John Prescott

THE LONGRIDERS
THE HARD ONE

TOR

A TOM DOHERTY ASSOCIATES BOOK
NEW YORK

THE LONGRIDERS

Copyright © 1954 by Stadium Publishing Corp. First published in *Best Western*. Reprinted by permission of the author and Scott Meredith Literary Agency, Inc., 845 Third Avenue, New York, N.Y. 10022.

THE HARD ONE

Copyright © 1953 by Stadium Publishing Corp. First published in *Complete Western Book* as "The Hard One They All Hated." Reprinted by permission of the author and Scott Meredith Literary Agency, Inc., 845 Third Avenue, New York, N.Y. 10022.

Compilation copyright © 1990 by Tor Books

A Tor Book
Published by Tom Doherty Associates, Inc.
49 West 24th St.
New York, NY 10010

Cover art by Ballestar

ISBN: 0-812-50544-1

First edition: December 1990

Printed in the United States of America

0 9 8 7 6 5 4 3 2 1

THE LONGRIDERS

• CHAPTER 1 •
Shotgun on Top

WHEN THE THREE RIDERS CAME INTO THE DIP A FEW yards from the scarred and twisted road, they dismounted and sent their horses around behind a jutting stand of fractured rocks. The first two slumped down on the gravel with their shoulders against a boulder and their hats tipped back, and Alec Winton stepped out into the road and cocked his head toward the south.

"Nothin' yet, Stone," he said. He took off his hat, batted it against his thigh and put it on again as he sat down. "Quiet as can be."

"We're early," Stone said. "And if we wasn't it wouldn't make no difference either. That thing ain't been on time since it begun to run."

"Be nice if it was," Alec said. "I sure do hate sittin' around in this heat. I hope they got somethin' with 'em besides money. I hope they got a drink of water, maybe. How about that, Pike?"

The boy named Pike turned his smooth face and

smiled. When Pike sat quiet and relaxed like that Alec thought he looked a good deal younger than he really was.

"Or whiskey," Pike said. "It sure would beat that alcohol and water we got back in camp."

"You ain't goin' to drink no more," Stone said quietly. "I'll bat your ears off if'n you do; even good whiskey, you ain't." Stone picked up a rock and heaved it at a yucca.

Alec smiled pleasantly at Stone Johnson. "You ain't goin' to bat no one's ears off," he said.

Stone stood up and shook himself all over. Standing with his legs slightly spread and with his hat still angled, Stone looked to Alec like he might be made of granite. Stone was big without being tall and he had no shape to his body at all. He was just square and solid all the way to the top of his rusty, unkempt hair. Even his face was like that; a man never knew from Stone's face what was going on behind it. It was simply flat and without expression, except for his eyes, which were so small and so far back beneath his brows that a man had to look sharp to catch anything going on in there.

Stone looked at Alec for a moment, then went into the road and stood motionless, his head tipped. He raised one hand slightly the way a music teacher might when she wants to hear a certain note again, then he dropped it and shambled back to them. Stone never hurried.

"Horse comin'," he said. "Down the road."

"Isidro," Alec said. Alec stood up, loosened the gun again and peered around the boulder between them and the road.

"Damn fool ought to hit the brush," Stone said behind him. "Won't do to have all that dust in the air."

"It's all right," Alec said. "The wind'll take it off; he knows enough to keep ahead of 'em some."

Alec turned around and saw Stone scowling off across the road and brush on the other side to where the hazy Guadeloupes shook and trembled far away. When Stone got his back up about something a body never knew which direction he was going to move in. Just now, that thing about Pike had got him to eating on Isidro.

"I guess you and me better stay here and let Pike and Isidro go down and cover on the side and rear," Alec said to Stone.

Stone kept staring at the distant mountains. "Rather cover the rear myself," he said; then his eyes came around to Alec. "I'll take Isidro, you can have the kid."

Alec said, "All right," easily and let it ride. He went around behind the rocks to get his horse, coming back as Isidro pounded into the dip from the road in a ball of dust and high-flung gravel. Isidro's hat was lying on his neck and his round, dark face was split in the whiteness of his smile. Isidro talked rapidly without dismounting.

"She's coming now; she's coming here in only a minute," he said.

"How many?" Alec said. "How many horses—the hitch?"

"Caballos? Oh, four. Si, four—and two men on top. I think there are maybe four or five inside."

"Outriders?" Stone Johnson said.

Isidro laughed. "No; none of those. But a shotgun—yes, a shotgun on top."

"Must be some money, then, anyway," Stone said. Stone walked behind the rock and nobody said anything until he returned with his horse. "Come on, then," Stone said. "We better get on with it. You foller me, Isidro."

Isidro swung his horse around to track Stone into the brush beyond the road, then paused and raised his eyebrows at Alec, who nodded at him.

"Go ahead," Alec said. "Pike'll stay here. Don't get too far down there, and keep out of sight." He raised his voice slightly at Stone's thick neck. "You hear, Stone? Don't get anxious."

The two riders were disappearing into the brush as Pike came around the boulder on his horse. Pike was pulling his old Sharps out of the saddle scabbard as Alec climbed aboard.

"Put that thing away, Pike," he said. "You won't need it."

Pike laughed and held the rifle across the saddle in front of him. "If I know Stone, I will. He's got a mind to start a ruckus down there and then I'll have to get the shotgun 'afore we all get blowed up. What's in his craw, anyway?"

"He's just bein' himself, that's all." Alec let his eyes wander up the foothills of the Guadeloupes, then let them drift around to Pike. "He's sore 'cause you drunk yourself into a scrap in that Carlsbad honkytonk the other night and we had to fight our way out of town."

"Never knew him to mind a fight before," Pike said. Pike sat easily and smiled at Alec. "He starts plenty of 'em, and then we got to give him a hand."

"Yeah, well, he likes to pick his own," Alec said. " 'Sides, he had a girl there he was makin' up to. You kind of ruined that."

They were quiet for a moment and Alec could hear the sound of the horses and the stage coming toward them. The road twisted and writhed along the shattered and broken landscape, now plunging through arroyos and defiles and now lying flat upon the level ground. Following the road, the growing noise was sometimes loud and near at hand, and then again was muted as a cholla or mesquite patch or a rock formation intervened.

"You ain't sore at me, are you, Alec?" Pike said in one of the silent places. Pike had edged up beside

Alec and Alec could see the fine muscles setting in his facial structure.

"No, I ain't sore at you, Pike. Just be careful, that's all. We're all in this thing together; we can't be stirrin' up trouble amongst ourselves."

Alec was watching young Pike's face and for a moment it seemed that Pike was going to say something again, but then he didn't because the stage came out of the last turn and the clattering and pounding hooves were near and loud. At the same time, the gunfire commenced to rattle and Alec knew that Stone was doing just what Pike had said he would.

He always lost track of detail and the sequence of individual incidents in a thing like that and he was already in the road and driving the spurs before he was aware of making up his mind to do it. The stage was a hundred yards away, swaying crazily with the driver standing and with the shotgun bent around the seat trying to get a look into the plume of dust behind them. Alec could not yet find Isidro or Stone, but he could hear the shooting and he knew that Stone was having a fine time boring the carriage with his bullets. Stone always liked to imagine the passengers jumping around all over one another.

Then the driver got his eyes on them and Alec saw him shouting at the shotgun, which swerved around just as young Pike raised the Sharps and fired. The big gun went off right alongside Alec's head, nearly caving in his eardrum; he felt the hot, staggering concussion and the breath of flame, and saw the shotgun straighten up, then double and pitch forward in the traces.

It all changed after that and the fight went out of the driver. He commenced to saw on the reins and then he leaned back and threw his weight against the bits. He was bent nearly flat when the stage began to weave and slow, with the horses tossing wild and white-eyed against the pressure on their mouths. The dust began to flatten out behind the stage and Alec saw Stone and Isidro riding to the rear of it. They were pressed in close and yelling, and Isidro caught the rear boot and swung on up as Alec threw the weight of his horse against the carriage lead, forcing the animals into the beginning of an arc.

The driver stood in the front boot with his hands raised and his face sick-yellow from sight of the mess dangling in the traces until Alec ordered him down. Isidro was on top, systematically throwing the dunnage down and young Pike covered the whole proceedings with the terrible Sharps. Stone dismounted slowly and jerked the door of the carriage open.

Isidro had been right about the number of occupants, Alec saw; there were five all right, but now two of them were squashed flat and oddly shapeless in one corner and on the floor. The other three came out as though they were in some kind of dream—two women, neat and shiny in Eastern silks and brocades, and a paunchy man with a small mustache and a grey face in which dark eyes rolled hugely. The two women stood stiff and numb, their gloved fingers writhing in amongst each other, and the man leaned against the dusty stage with his thick hands curled above his head and his cheeks making puffy motions and his voice croaking in a language Alec did not understand.

"Non! Non! Mon Dieu!"

The strange-tongued man was staring with fascination at the Sharps in young Pike's hands, and Pike laughed and swung the gun, barrel on, at him. That time the unknown language poured out in a torrent, and the tone of voice rose sharply.

"Mon Dieu, non! Pas de fusil!"

Stone moved in, grabbed the smooth folds of the fat man's vest and shook him against the carriage wall.

"What you sayin', there, dammit? Quit your howlin', you ain't hurt."

Pike laughed again and looked down curiously at the man Stone held against the stage.

"That's French he's talkin', Stone. That's French—my grandsir used to talk it around sometimes. He learnt it from them French trappers that used to come into the mountains for beaver and the like."

Stone let his hand drop and stepped back, studying the fat man as he might regard an unusual and seldom-seen animal.

"French, huh? Can't he speak white? American?"

Pike screwed up his face, thinking hard. Then he said, "Parley-vous . . . parley-vous American? Spik English?"

The Frenchman's eyes were hard on Pike and Alec thought his face shone like a light when he heard his native tongue. His hand made a fluttering, appealing motion as he talked. "Mais, oui! Je parle Anglais un peu. Some. Attendez! I speak some—un peu."

Pike grinned at Stone when the Frenchman stopped. "Say, that ain't bad, is it? I reckon I could be a regular interpreter if I wanted to."

"I still can't make sense out 'o what he's sayin'," Stone said. He spat into the dust at the Frenchman's feet, and one of the women commenced to weep, her face lugubrious in distortion.

When Stone's attention turned to the women, Alec commenced to poke among the sacks and boxes which Isidro was throwing down from the carriage roof and boots. It sure was funny what people'd lug around with them, he was thinking. Himself, now, he liked to travel light. It ought to be enough for a person to have a suit of clothes, maybe, a pair of shoes or boots and maybe a change of underwear; but there sure weren't no need for all the riggin' people were bringin' into the country nowadays. Pretty nearly every stage they hit lately was loaded down with the kind of clothes and frills no knowing person would give storage space to out here.

Them women there, they was probably school-marms or the like. Couldn't be girls for none of the honkytonks up the line—didn't have the right kind of faces in the first place and more'n likely didn't have the legs neither, though a man couldn't tell about that with their dresses dragging down along the ground the way they did.

And that Frenchman—he was no doubt some kind of trader or traveler out here poking into this or that—though he was a blame fool to come out this way without he knew how to talk like any other person. Still, them foreigners were a foxy lot sometimes; if they had enough money they didn't need to talk—everybody understood the language money had. Like that English feller that'd got the Lincoln war a-goin'; 'course he spoke straight and you could pretty nearly always understand him, but even so it wasn't regular talk. Except the money part of it.

When Isidro whooped and threw the first bottle down, Alec caught it in his hands and unwrapped the straw from the smooth, green glass. Inside, a transparent liquid filled the bottle nearly to the top, too light for whiskey, but then again too lively to be water. There was a strange-appearing label on the side of it and Alec looked at the Frenchman and held the bottle up.

The Frenchman's eyes were those of a pleading dog and he said something unintelligible. Alec gave the bottle to Pike and Pike stared at it and laboriously phrased a question. That time the Frenchman became voluble and made waving gestures with his hands.

"It's a kind of wine," Pike said. "It's something he calls champagne and he brought it all the way out here to sell it."

"Wine, huh," Alec said. He took the bottle from Pike and smashed the neck on the rim of one of the carriage wheels. The liquid became a sudden, foaming gusher and Alec put the jagged glass to his lips quick. Inside his mouth, the effervescent bubbles tickled his palate and got around into the back end of his nose and made him sneeze.

He wiped his mouth with the back of his hand and passed the bottle to Pike, who took a long drink and smacked his lips. Then Stone came out of the stage with his hands bloody from feeling in the pockets of the dead men, and took the bottle from Pike. When he pulled it away from his mouth he stared at it and Alec looked at the Frenchman. Big tears were rolling down the flat and flabby face.

"What's his trouble?" Stone said. Stone was grinning and he took another long drink and kept his eyes on the Frenchman's face.

"I guess he don't figure we ought to be drinkin' that stuff without we pay for it," Pike said. "He must have a heap of money tied up in it."

"Then it must be pretty good," Stone said. Stone tipped the bottle up once more and then he turned it up and laughed as the remaining drops dribbled on the ground. He was laughing with his head back and his far-back eyes mean and happy.

Alec saw it all and he could have stopped it, maybe, but he didn't; there was something wrong about a grown man making tears over a possession of any kind, and it wouldn't let him move. He saw how the Frenchman was looking like a sacrilege had been committed, how his face went white and stiff and his eyes big and crazy as he swung out from the carriage. The Frenchman's voice was piping in a wild tumble of words and his hands were beating in fat, weird blows at Stone's face and chest. When Stone stepped back, drew and fired into the round, full paunch the sound was all the sound in the world, and the Frenchman fell straight down and lay flat with no gestures.

• CHAPTER 2 •
False Trail

THE FIRE WAS RED HOT AND THE APACHE LAID THE PI-ñon log in butt first, Indian-fashion. The underside caught quickly from the low blaze of the coal bed and carried on down to the point where it passed beyond the ring of the pit. There was a fine smell to piñon smoke and Alec took a deep breath of it.

"It sure is nice to come back to something like this, ain't it, Pike?" he said.

"Yeah, a man works up an appetite climbin' his horse up here; and a thirst, too." Pike rolled over and raised himself to one elbow; he hoisted the champagne bottle and drank with noisy swallows.

Alec leaned back against his saddle, his fingers formed upon the firmness of another one of the bottles, and gazed across the fire at the mess of meat the Apache had laid out on the bark sheets.

"I hope it ain't beef again," he said idly. "A man gets tired of eatin' beef all the time, even if he don't have to grow it and feed it hisself."

"It's a nice couple of fawns," Stone said. Stone was sitting across the fire and his face was soft and friendly from the flames and the wine. Stone had gotten around to thinking the French wine was pretty good; he'd even expressed a regret that he'd shot the paunchy man before he'd found out where to get some more of it. "I figure a nice couple of fawns'll go good with this here wine; almost like a regular fiesta."

"Fiesta?" Isidro came out of the bushes on the fringe of the darkness and looked at Stone. "Where is this fiesta, Stone?"

"Right here, amigo; we got our own private fiesta right up here in the Guadeloupes. Ain't you listenin' to what we're sayin'?"

"I was in the bushes," Isidro said, smiling. Isidro buckled his belt and walked around the fire to the wooden cases on the ground. He pulled a bottle out of one of them, threw the straw into the fire and began to pry at the cork with his knife.

Stone chuckled with a private amusement, then laughed aloud. "Use your teeth, Isidro—you're the only one that's got any."

Pike sat up suddenly and said, "That ain't so, Stone. Look at mine." Pike bared his white teeth in a wide grimace and even tugged at a few of them with his fingers to carry out his point. "See there, Stone? They're stuck in there just like trees. I ain't got but a couple of loose ones and they're way back."

Pike pried further into his mouth to show exactly where these were and Alec got up and walked around the fire, crouching down at the two mounds beneath the blankets. He bent over one of them and shook the outline of a shoulder gently.

"Clint," he said. "You awake? How you feelin'?"

The man named Clint rolled over and looked up at Alec. The thin face was harsh and sharply defined in the light of the fire, and it made Alec think that

Clint's bones had too much edge on them and that they were too close to his skin. Even beneath the bandage around his head, they protruded, like the spikes of his raggedly cropped hair, which jutted through the folds of cloth.

"I got a devil of a headache," Clint said. "I feel like some critter been kickin' at me all day long."

Alec separated the bandage with his fingers and looked at the angry crease on Clint's head. The blood was caked and hard and Clint winced when a thread, imbedded in the crust, commenced to pull.

"I guess maybe you ought to stay like this for a couple days yet," Alec said. "We won't be doin' nothin' for awhile."

"I want to go out on the next one," Clint said. "The Apache ain't no company, and Roy, there, he ain't much neither."

The other blanket moved and the man beneath it struggled and sat up, one arm hugged to his chest. "That's 'cause I talk too intelligent for your simple mind," Roy said. Roy's wide face smiled at Alec, his far-apart eyes reflecting the fire which splashed his red face. Roy's face always looked as though his mind might be a word or two behind whatever conversation might be going around him at the moment. "How'd it go, Alec?"

"All right," Alec said. "A little over a thousand in hard money and greenbacks, five cases of French wine." Alec looked over at Stone before he went on. "And four defuntos."

Clint got his elbows beneath him and pushed up. "Four? You must 'a sure enough had a scrap."

"Didn't need to be any, except maybe the shotgun," Alec said. "Stone had one of his spells."

Clint was sitting nearly straight up now and his eyes were bright with the vicarious living of Stone's slaughter. "Four, huh; he get 'em all?"

Alec moved over to Roy and looked at his arm.

"No, Pike got the shotgun," he said. "Stone did for the others; gut-shot one of 'em." Roy's arm was fat with the dressing on it and Alec didn't fool with it. When he got to his knees the Apache was standing over him. The Apache's face was dark and impassive, even with the fire on it.

"Yerba," he said, and he patted his arm.

Roy looked up and laughed. "Yerba, yerba, that's all he says. He goes off in the brush and comes back with a mess 'o weeds and packs that on the arm and says, 'yerba'." Roy grinned into the face of the renegade. "But, hang it all, it feels good. Ain't hardly no pain any more at all."

"I guess them yerbas are the stuff, then," Alec said.

Alec glanced toward the Apache again, but he was no longer there. In one slick movement he returned to the fire, squatted on his blanket, brought a piece of the fawn meat to his mouth and sliced it off at his lips with a white flick of his knife-blade. The whole thing was as quiet and smooth as the motion of a shadow and Alec stared hard.

"Stone got three all at once," Clint was marveling, and Alec turned his head toward him again. Clint was looking at the fire, his young mouth curved smoothly and his eyes bright and happy-mean the way that Stone's would get.

"You better ask him," Alec said. "I ain't sure how he did it—except the one he gut-shot."

Alec stood up and walked back to his saddle again.

They were mostly quiet for a time because the fawn-meat was tender and succulent, and not the least bit gamey, and there was enough of the French wine to keep everybody occupied. Alec backed his shoulders against the saddle, shoved his legs out in front of him and let the fire's heat toast the bottoms of his boots. Inside, the wine was fuzzing in his head and lifting his weariness away. The tiny bubbles were prancing around in his mouth and throat the way that no kind of whiskey had ever done and likely never would. It was an entirely new sensation and one he took a huge enjoyment in. It seemed to make him loose and airy all over; it seemed to give his arms and legs, and head even, an independence of the rest of his body—like they could maybe go off somewhere on their own if they pleased.

Lying back with his face turned skyward, Alec thought the stars were very near. The pines and cedars, rising up on either side, made a kind of cone, and the few stars in there were bright and almost close enough to touch. It made him think again how fine it was to live out in the open like they did; how fine and clean it was to go where they pleased and live off the land or on the wild game the Apache might shoot for them. It made him think how it might never have happened that way at all if it hadn't been for the Lincoln war up north a bit.

Take Pike, there, or Isidro—they were pretty much alike, though Pike was a mountain man and God only knew where Isidro'd come from. But they were similar just the same, and if they hadn't got into the cattle war and become outlaws because of it, they'd like as not be looping their riatas over a beef herd, or dragging themselves around the countryside behind a plow. Isidro, anyway; maybe Pike wouldn't. Bein' from the mountain country, Pike might try to make a go of trapping like his grandsir did, though there wasn't much to that these days. Nor hide huntin' neither—so that big old Sharps, which he wouldn't nohow trade or sell for a Winchester, wouldn't be good for nothin' but to drag him down. And he might have wound up behind a plow, too; or anyway herdin' a bunch of beef around, and crackin' piñones in front of the fire with his woman in the evening.

Stone, now, he never would have done a thing like

that if he'd lived to be a thousand and so the war was made to order for him; and, yes, maybe for Clint, too, and Roy. Them three were pretty well whacked out of the same bolt of cloth, though Roy and Clint weren't up to Stone's color yet, even if they sometimes liked to think they were—especially Clint liked to think he was.

Whatever made Stone the kind of man he was, was sort of hard to figure out, and it didn't always pay to go snooping in amongst his private thoughts with questions and the like. Feller like him more than likely had some bitter thing occur to him a great while back, that twisted him and made him hostile to his kind, and gave him a taste for human blood, no matter what the circumstances.

Almost like the Apache in that respect. Didn't make no difference that the renegade hadn't put his knife in anyone since he'd high-tailed it away from Geronimo's crowd. A man only had to catch him making his incantations over his war bundle—to see him fondle them tired old sacred eagle feathers, and get a glimpse of a few of them musty scalps he kept in with the feathers—to know what was goin' through his mind. He never did nothin' but hunt and do the cookin' and camp chores, and never even spoke but half a dozen words, but that didn't make no difference. A body only had to sneak a look at his face when Stone was braggin' of his killin's. Like tonight—the renegade's eyes had glittered bright as a pair of fancy diamond rings. There wasn't another of his features moved, or even flickered, but them eyes told everything there was to say.

When he got to thinking about the Apache Alec turned his head slightly to look at him and he saw Pike Forey's face close up to him, and curious. Pike smiled when he saw Alec wasn't asleep.

"I guess I was just thinkin' with my eyes closed,"

Alec said. "All that French wine just shut 'em up and I didn't even know it."

"Goes to a man's head, all right," Pike said. "Can't say I ever had anything like it before. Sure is nice." Pike paused and looked away into the darkness in the general direction of the Pecos, many miles away. Then he said, "Alec, where do you reckon them folks were goin'?"

Alec rolled his head easily in the cradle of his hands and looked straight up at the stars. "Folks, Pike? What folks you talkin' about?" And then he remembered the stage coming from the south, and he said, "Those folks. Oh, them; why, like as not they was headin' up for Carlsbad or Artesia, or maybe Roswell or even Fort Sumner. Hard to tell, seein' as how we didn't ask 'em."

"There's a lot of their likes comin' in now, ain't there?" Pike said quietly. "I mean folks that look like their aim is to be nesters or settlers, or maybe set up in some kind of trade in the towns."

"Yeah," Alec said. "There's a lot, all right. Times change—even out here where nobody thought they ever would. Who'd ever suppose we'd one day be drinkin' this champagne."

Pike sat up and crossed his legs beneath him, his face becoming eager. "That's just what I mean. And that ain't only the beginnin'. People like we saw to-day comin' in; people in brought-on clothes. And others in big wagons piled high with bedding and pots and pans and smoothed-down painted furniture even; and some bringin' milk cows tied on behind."

"Yeah, there's a new crowd, all right." Alec was listening carefully to Pike, but it was the tone of voice rather than the content of his talk that was commanding to his interest. It made Alec remember that Pike would likely never be with them here if the cattle war had not come along.

"I even saw a new fence the other day," Pike went

on, almost shyly. "Down near the river. One of them bob-wire ones, all shiny and stretchin' along the ground as straight as an arrow. Feller was plowin' up the ground for somethin' or other, and he had a new house built—not much, but a house just the same."

Listening to Pike ramble on, Alec let his eyes wander around the camp. The fire had been allowed to die down some and the shadows were creeping into the open glade. Stone and Clint and Roy were lying beneath their blankets, sleeping, and Isidro was putting the empty bottles back in the cases. The first time his eyes went around he saw the Apache licking his knife and sticking it into his sheath and wiping his hands on his leggings, but when they came around again the Apache was standing up, with his head tilted toward the crowns of the trees.

He stood that way for maybe several seconds, motionless and deep-colored, like a smoothly carved and polished cedar block, and then he walked beyond the perimeter of the fire and dropped on all fours and put the side of his head against the ground. When Isidro went over to him and crouched beside him he lifted his head and they talked together for a moment, the Apache's voice hoarse and far down in his chest. Then he pressed his head to the ground again, and Isidro hopped up and came quickly around the fire.

"Something coming," Isidro said, hunkering down beside Alec and Pike. "The Apache hears horses coming up the hills. There are quite a few, he says."

Isidro was smiling as though the Apache's message was the signal for a pleasant game and Alec sprang to his feet and ran around the fire with Isidro and Pike behind him. The renegade looked up, grunted and shook his head and waved his arm vaguely in the direction of the steep slope toward the Pecos and the valley.

"Horses," he said. "Many horses come."

"Horses?" Alec said. "Coming here? At night?"

"Sí, yes, horses," Isidro put in. "Many of them. He hear them in the ground. They are coming for certain."

The Apache was no longer paying any attention to them and Alec broke away and pushed through the brush and weaved among the trees to the clear space where the rocks fell away toward the valley far below. It was very dark out there, and even the stars, which hung in clusters for as far as he could see— to the end of the world, it seemed—failed to illuminate the depth of blackness. He was standing in a great cave, and seeing nothing.

Isidro was puffing with exertion when he came up beside him and stood with his hands on his hips and his head cocked.

"Do you hear them? Do you see them? How can you see them in this black? It is looking into the belly of a black bear."

"No, I don't see 'em yet, or hear 'em," Alec said. "But if the Apache says they're comin' then they're comin'. Even at night."

Alec squatted on the bare rock and waited for Isidro to join him before he spoke again. Then he said, "Apache put the fire out?"

"Sí, yes," Isidro said. "He putting it out now; and bringing the horses in." Isidro scratched his head and stared hard into the night below them. "It is Stone who do this, no?"

"Yeah, Stone did it, I reckon. Don't figure on a night chase—especially up into a place like this— 'less they're real upset, like they must be now. If Stone had used his head and not done so much blood-lettin' maybe they wouldn't 'a come."

"I think they very angry down there," Isidro said. "To come up here like this at night. The Apache says there are many."

"Yeah, they must'a got the whole blame country out of bed. No right-minded man'd give a thing like this a thought 'till morning, but the people 'round here seem to be changin'; rush headlong into anythin'."

Isidro grunted, but otherwise said nothing, and Alec pushed to his feet. "Can't tell nothin' yet," he said. "Too far off, I guess. You better stay here for awhile, though. I got to get the others up and ready."

"Si," Isidro said. "I stay here; I call when I hear them come."

"All right—no, better not do that; you just come on back and we'll clear out. Just try and get their direction. That's enough."

Alec went back to the clearing and saw Pike and the Apache helping Roy and Clinton onto their horses. The fire was very dim, and scarcely glowing, but it was enough to define the shape of Stone still humped and quiet beneath his blanket. Alec walked across the ground and kicked him in the buttocks.

"Come on, Stone, pile out. We got a ride comin' up, thanks t'you."

Stone shifted his position ponderously and Alec kicked him again. "Stone. Get up, Stone. We got to ride; move your bones."

That time Stone rolled over and opened his eyes. They fell on Alec, moved vaguely around, then focused on Alec again. "Who you kickin'?" he said. "Who you think you're kickin'?"

"I'm kickin' you, Stone. Come on. Roll out. We got a posse on our necks. We got to get out."

Stone rolled over on his belly, got his knees and arms beneath him and pushed. He rose slowly with one hand to his head, and Alec steadied him as he wavered on his feet.

"Go on, Stone, pile on. The Apache's got your horse ready."

Stone's hand dropped from his head and he stood

precariously with his legs wide, gazing stupidly at the saddled horses and the embers of the dying fire. He shook his head dully and turned around slowly. "Posse? What posse's that?"

"The one that's comin' for us," Alec said. "The one you brought on with all your killin' at the stage."

Stone's eyes were so far back and obscure in his head that they appeared as a straight line of black across the upper part of his face. He was bending slightly forward, as though his body was losing balance, or gathering strength for a sudden movement. Alec's hand glided toward his gun.

It seemed to Alec that they stood that way, facing each other, with the slow enmity acquiring a physical quality in the air between them, for a great while. He was conscious of the alert and nervous quiet in the others. Roy and Clint were watching closely from their horses; the renegade was standing motionless just beyond the fire pit, and Pike was pausing with a foot in the stirrup, one hand grasping the bridle and the other reaching for the cantle of his saddle. Then they all relaxed as Isidro came through the bushes and made loud noises when he saw what was occurring.

"I hear them coming now," he said, and he shouldered into the space between Stone and Alec, though he spoke to all of them. "They are far off, but I hear the horses stepping on the rocks. They are surely coming this way."

"All right, get goin' then, that's too close," Alec said. He slapped Isidro's shoulder and spun him half around with a push toward the horses. "We'll have to lay a false trail somehow."

The sudden change in current caught Stone in its rush and propelled him toward the horse the Apache held. Alec swung up quickly to his own and waited until the Apache had buried the fire completely before he spoke again.

"Pike, you get 'em out of here," he said then. "Keep north and go steady. Stone'll stay with me; we'll find you soon."

In the depth of darkness Clint's voice was eager. "I'm stayin' too, Alec. I'm fightin' with Stone."

"No, you ain't, Clint," Alec said. "You're goin'. We can't be dogged by no hurt men."

Then leather creaked, horses snorted and stomped as Pike got the group moving out; Pike passed close for a quick squeeze of Alec's arm and Isidro swung up before tagging after the others.

"Adios, amigo, we see you when the coyote cries." The smell of the wine was thick in Isidro's breathing as he bent close to Alec's head. "Have care," he added softly. "It is not always simple to know whether one's enemies are to the front or to the rear."

"I'll watch it," Alec said, and it became slowly quiet as the brush bent and whispered with the movement of the animals; and returned to place when they had gone. Only Stone was noising into the silence, still dizzy an thick from the wine and sleep.

"I don't take to that kickin', Alec," he was saying. "Ain't nobody can do that to me."

"I had to wake you, Stone," Alec said. "Wasn't much time to croon you into life."

"I ain't listenin' to you, Stone, but keep on yappin' anyway. It's as good a way as any to draw 'em to us."

• CHAPTER 3 •
The Trooper

THEY SAT THEIR HORSES IN THE CLEARING FOR QUITE awhile, Alec now and then prodding Stone with some remark or other to keep him going; then, when the posse seemed to be getting close enough they made a great flurry and crashing in the brush before going over the rim and back toward the valley. A night posse's only advantage lay in the element of surprise, and when that failed it had always been Alec's experience that nothing was so discouraging as leading it back to where it had come from.

The going was steep and treacherous, and though they were compelled to move slowly it did not bother Alec. Whatever ground they covered would have to be traveled by the posse in its turn and he knew its familiarity with the slope was less than his and that their numbers would slow them down. To make certain that they did not lose the posse altogether he would fire at it now and then, just to whet the collective appetites and to keep the interest up. Nevertheless, the whole thing was a needless inconvenience, and Stone's stupidity got Alec angrier every minute.

A body'd think that a man who lived by his gun and wits would have more sense than to indulge in a lot of pointless butchery, but that seemed to appeal to Stone more than anything else. That killer instinct had been a mighty handy thing in the Lincoln fight, and Alec had always been glad to have Stone and Clint and Roy around in those days, but with this kind of living it was sometimes more embarrassing than valuable. Stone never gave a hang for anything as long as he had a skull to drill.

The trouble was that Stone had no sense of proportion, and his mulish streak was too strong to let him listen to anyone that had. Stone, now, he couldn't see the changing times and that the people coming in around the Pecos there weren't the kind to scare quick and give up like they'd always done when Stone had gotten wild before. The day was pretty near gone when he could swagger through a town with Clint and Roy tagging on behind him, acting as he pleased and making a holy terror of himself. For all their fancy clothes, and storekeepin' and plowin' of the lowlands, the new town folk and valley nesters was a stubborn lot and Stone had got to learn that for himself some time.

After a bit, the late moon began to ease up over Mescalero Ridge far, far away, and they could move a little faster. They were down below the sheer rock cliffs by then, and coming into the lower foothills where the ground was somewhat clearer and undulating rather than cleft and shattered. The rising moon gave an eerie quality to everything around them, increasing the depth of shadow where it didn't reach, and making rocks and gravel and yes, even brush, shine brightly where it did. It seemed to give a ghostly luminescence to those many things, which they never had at any other time.

When they were a few miles south of the Black— still west of the Pecos—the moon was higher and Alec knew there wasn't much danger of the posse losing sight of them as long as they didn't try to evade it for awhile. Isidro and the others had an hour or more on the trail by now, but Alec thought they ought to keep the posse occupied for a bit more time.

"I figure that bunch back there's been havin' it too easy," Stone said presently. Stone was beginning to come around and appreciate what they'd gotten into. "We ought to hole up around here somewhere and set a trap maybe."

"It'd just be enough to discourage 'em some," Alec said, "but I figured we'd wait 'till we reached the Black. Better cover for one thing, and if need be we can go either up or down the stream if the posse gets bothersome." Alec stood up in his stirrups and tried to locate the dark trench of the Black ahead of them. "Ain't much chance of the horses gettin' hit, nei- ther."

Stone turned around in his saddle and gave a long look behind them before he said anything again. Stone was waking up, now, and taking a lively inter- est in everything that was going on.

"Must be ten or so from what I can tell from here," he said after a minute. "Can't be sure, though. What d'you think?"

"Can't tell for sure either," Alec said. "Dang moon makes everything look crazy. Ten anyhow. Count on a dozen, though." He stood up and peered ahead again. "Black's comin' up now. Quarter of a mile."

Maybe it was the moon lifting higher and making the shadows shorter and less misleading, or maybe the posse had seen the Black as well, but either way the guns back there commenced to whack away and Alec heard the lead sing overhead. The ground before them was rolling and clear and Alec set the spurs in deep. He was beginning to feel the excitement that a chase like that always gave to him and when he glanced at Stone he heard Stone's laughter rising above the thunder of the hooves.

At the Black, they braked down the rubble slope to the shallow water, dismounted out of sight of the ground above them and crawled up the bank and lay flat with their Winchesters. Alec could hear the posse very plainly, and presently he could see it again, lifting up the slow rise of ground, pausing, then breaking out in a wide arc in front of them. Stone swore and took his hat off.

"Damn it, they ain't supposed to do that," he said. "They ain't supposed to know nothin' about that kind of stuff at all."

"Seems they got some schoolin' on it somewhere, though," Alec said. Alec stared hard at the flankers, moving smudges in the queer light, then brought his eyes in toward the center, where a small knot was just dispersing. The big blot broke up and the individuals melted away before his eyes. In another moment, the rolling land was clear of any life.

Lord, how quiet it was! A body'd think there'd be some kind of sound around there. A body'd think that, with all the life there was in the rocks, there, and the brush, and creeping about in the holes and burrows in the soil, there'd be some kind of sound. You'd think the wild things'd be out skulking about for nourishment; you'd think the coyotes'd be sitting up there in the rocks, bawling away at the moon, so big and dead, the way they always seemed to do when a body was tryin' to get a wink of sleep. You'd even think there might be a bird or two hanging around to see what all the commotion had been about before it got as silent as it was.

But everything was just as lifeless as though the Lord had never put a living thing upon the earth at all; Alec's voice seemed so loud to him that it was startling, and without knowing exactly why, he dropped it to a whisper.

"A fine trap this is," he said without taking his eyes away from the silent land. "Looks almost like we're gettin' caught in it ourselves."

"Who'd ever figger them nesters'd think of doin' a thing like that." Stone said. "No farmer'd ever have that much sense."

"Like I said, they got schoolin' in it somehow. You see how a few of them gathered there in the middle like they was gettin' directions?"

"I seen it," Stone said. Stone levered a cartridge into the chamber of the Winchester and the action crashed in the quiet. "Maybe we should 'a let 'em have it then, 'ceptin' they wasn't supposed to know what we was doin'. How did they?"

Alec looked at Stone and saw that he was smiling; he saw that Stone was enjoying it and was just as happy that they'd been trapped themselves. It made him think that Stone was the best to have with him in a place like this; Stone who never rattled or got excited, who never gave a hang for anything as long as there was killing to be had. There was some good in Stone, at that.

"They just must'a known we'd do this," Alec said. "Someone among 'em been thinkin' right along with us, figurin' we'd most likely drop in here for a spell, and was set for it."

"Ain't no vigilante posse got someone who can think like that," Stone said. Stone was still smiling, speaking through his teeth while his eyes roamed along the land.

"This one has," Alec said, "and I'm thinkin' we better get a move on. We can't do much with 'em spread out like this, and gettin' wider every minute."

Stone's voice was soft with banter when he answered. "Alec—Alec, you ain't gettin' scared, are ya?

You ain't goin' to let a bunch of nesters run you out, are ya?"

This was the bad part of Stone—one of them—the part that had no sense; Alec was very careful, like he was explaining something to a little boy. "They may be nesters, just like you say, but they got a mind tellin' 'em what to do. This ain't no bunch that can be scattered like we figured."

Alec kept his eyes on Stone and in a little while he could tell that he was beginning to make an impression. A man had to beat on Stone with a gun-butt sometimes, but if he kept it up something was bound to give. Stone's brows commenced to frown, some, above his deep-set eyes.

"I figure we better work up the river," Alec went on. "We might run into the flankers up in there, but we won't have the whole bunch on our necks. Them rocks'll give us better cover, too, but we got to get to 'em before they do."

Stone was quiet for a moment and Alec watched his face. There was never a way of knowing what was going on behind those blunt, flat features. A man never knew if logic was prevailing over the primitive forces motivating Stone's actions. Finally Stone slid down the bank and cradled the Winchester in his arm.

"All right, I don't like dry-gulchin' neither," he said; then he turned around and grinned. "Except when I'm doin' it. C'mon, let's go."

They led their horses through the water quietly. It was fairly deep at that point and at that time of year—too early for the summer drought—and the little ripples formed Vees around the horses' knees as they moved along, their hooves remaining below the surface.

At a point not far ahead, the stone monadnocks crashed high against the sky behind them. They didn't look to be more than a hundred yards away, two at the most, though Alec knew the moonlight could be deceptive in that respect. Sometimes a man could go ahead forever in the moonlight and never reach the point that he was heading for.

It was quiet, still, but not the kind of quiet there had been before. It seemed now that the night things were going on about their business, prowling through the brush and stone, squirming in their holes. Far away, in the high hills over west, a coyote sang a love song at the moon, and nearby, a bird swooped along the river bank, dipped down to scoop a bug from a quiet shallow, and rose on up to blend with the darkness overhead. Alec always felt a strange, tugging wonder when he saw a bird do that.

When the night split wide with sound and flame Alec and Stone were less than a hundred feet away from the rocks ahead. The sound crashed into the river bed and simultaneously with the shooting from above Alec was thrashing through the dragging water and returning the fire toward the sudden images which had appeared from the low cover on the bank. He was not at all conscious of his movements, or of those of Stone beside him, and there was even an element of surprise in seeing the Winchester sights before his eyes and watching one of the blurred figures spin away from the end of his gun barrel and drop down out of sight.

After that he was yelling at Stone and he could hear his voice shouting over and over again, "The rocks! Head for the rocks! The rocks, Stone!" He was yelling and running and feeling the awful drag of the water and trying to watch the bank of the river and the way ahead at the same time.

It was one of those times when he never seemed to cover an inch of ground at all. It seemed that he had been struggling toward the rocks since the beginning of time; and it seemed, too, that for every foot of distance he gained another foot was lost. He would never get there—he was sure of it. The murderous firing from the bank had died out from immediately beside them, but it was picking up again to their rear—the water churning in sudden, small spoutings and the ricochets screaming and caroming from the rising banks on either side. Once, his hat jerked at the chin cord, flipped to a rakish angle over his eyes; again, Stone stumbled ahead of him, swayed to his feet, the sleeve of one arm slowly darkening, then staining into the water-soaked cloth.

Alec caught up to Stone in a heave of energy, grasped him beneath his good arm and dragged his staggering bulk toward the rocks. They were very near, now; they were very near—as though they had never been as far away as they had seemed, or as though a few of the agonizing moments in time had been skipped over in his consciousness, and the rocks had crept benevolently closer to them in that interval.

Alec was breathing in gusts when he dragged Stone behind the first of the rocks and eased him to the ground. He removed a bandanna from his neck, wound it around Stone's arm, and tied it.

"Now, get out," he said. "Get your horse and ride; I'll hold this bunch back here."

Stone rolled over on his knees. He pressed his face against the rock with his eyes shut and breathed to the bottom of his lungs. Then he pushed himself away and fingered his arm.

"I ain't leavin'," he said. "This ain't nothin' but a crease. I ain't quittin'. I ain't quittin' never."

Almost, Alec could admire Stone in that moment. Almost, he felt a smile tugging at his lips, but then the memory of Stone's original stupidity was in his mind and stamped the good, warm feeling away. He put his knee on the Winchester, dropped his hand and his Colt slipped into his palm and fingers.

"I said to get out, Stone; I got no time to argue and explain about this."

Stone stared at the dull, dark barrel, then raised his eyes, uncomprehending. "You're puttin' a gun on me, Alec." Stone's voice was total disbelief.

"Damn right I am. I aim to get out of this mess and I can't do it if I've got you to stew about. How do I know you won't keel over—and I can't drag you all the way back to the Guadeloupes."

Alec rammed the Colt into Stone's belly and Stone jumped.

"Go on," he said. "Keep along the hills, there, and I'll find you. Take my water bottle with you; you'll have a thirst when that crease starts devilin' you in the mornin'."

With a slow movement, Stone stood up. Stone's face was like a hide stretched on a board for scraping. Every tendon and muscle in it was drawn as tight as one of the Apache's bowstrings.

Stone walked straight out of the rocks and waded into the water and took hold of the saddle pommel with both hands. He braced himself against it, jammed his boot into the stirrup, then sagged against the flank of the horse. Alec slid down the bank and when Stone heaved again Alec got his shoulder beneath his rump. Stone sat sluggishly and glared own at Alec.

"Damn your eyes, Alec, you're lucky you got that gun in your hand. Ain't nobody ever put a gun on me before, and lived."

"Nobody booted your pratt before either. Times change, Stone."

Alec backed off a pace or two, removed his water bottle from his saddle, and handed it up to Stone, who refused it.

"I don't want it," Stone said. "I don't need your filthy water; I'd rather eat sand or guzzle out o' some alkali hole."

Alec slipped the strap around Stone's pommel and Stone didn't seem to have the energy to take it off; he was using it all for swearing.

"Now git," Alec said. "Git on out so's I can look to the business at hand."

Stone made no move and Alec dipped the barrel of the gun and fired into the water at the horse's feet. The animal jumped and charged ahead; Stone tried to rein it in, but Alec fired again and that time the horse got out of Stone's hand and lunged up the bank. Stone bellowed back to Alec, insanely, once, then the horse was running wildly, and in another moment Alec could only hear them.

He went back up to the rocks, picked up the Winchester and flattened out on the ground beneath him. In the great and lonely quiet, Stone's horse was clattering loudly to the north and Alec watched the sloping ground before him, wondering if the sound of it would arouse the curiosity and impatience of the posse.

Maybe he should have kept Stone there—he could use another gun. Maybe he should have, but there was no telling yet how badly Stone was shot, and if he'd keeled over in a fight, or getaway, he'd have been a load to handle. Alec never cared too much for Stone, but he never would have left him to his own devices either, though he damn well deserved it this time.

Alec's eyes were lined up along the sights of the Winchester and pretty soon he saw a slow, cautious stirring in the brush far down along the river bed. Then there was another, not far from the first. These two rustlings and stirrings then became slow, shadowed movement—men—crawling toward each other to talk it over. A minute later, a third hunched up beside them. They were afoot, easy targets, but Alec held his fire.

Then across the slope of land, and down beyond his vision, there came the sound he had been anticipating. In the quiet the horses' walking carried far—must be half a dozen or so, Alec thought. They came up the slope in a careful walk, pausing just below the crest of it, where Alec could see the anonymous blob of movement in the brush and rubble. When one of the men in the first group stooped low and scatted toward the rise Alec knew that everything was ready. He dug his elbows in and laid the rifle stock against his cheek.

It came with a whoop and a holler and as the cavalcade cleared the rise and launched toward the rocks at a dead gallop Alec could feel the tremor in the ground against his belly. They were a hundred yards away and more, and yet with all the time available to him the sensation of facing what amounted to a cavalry charge made his stomach muscles knot and his saliva turn to sand. Before he should have, he commenced to lever brass.

After the first rounds the riders were much closer and everything had got a little mixed up. Everything seemed to speed up—to accelerate—to blend and merge, the sound of the shooting and the charging horses and the bravado-yelling and finally the shredded agony of horses plunging, shot and demented from their wounds. The charge commenced to waver, to lose its concentration, to spread. And when the ranks split the moon brought them out as individuals, and Alec found what he was looking for.

The leader rode a spotted grey, heavy in the flanks and broad and solid across the chest, and the moon brought him out in hammered silver. Low along the neck the rider pressed, his clothing dark and the bright sky shining on the short, peaked visor of his cap and the long streak of fire that was the saber in his hand. He was less than forty yards away when Alec brought his sights to bear; and his impetus was great enough to carry him nearly up to Alec's feet before he died beneath the floundering weight of his wounded horse. . . . Alec did not know then that he would always remember the chevronned sleeve, outstretched toward him, carrying the battle to the last.

• CHAPTER 4 •

Nothing but Nesters

IT WAS WELL AFTER SUNRISE WHEN ALEC FOUND STONE.
He had seen him a long way off, skirting the lifting
foothills, but he had come up with him slowly because there was no longer need to hurry. Anyway,
he was a little sick inside, and weighted with a kind
of strange and empty weariness that he'd never
known before. Near a cholla patch, Stone turned and
waited.

"Here's your water bottle," Stone said as Alec
reined up. "I ain't drunk a drop."

Alec took it, uncorked it and let the water run into
his mouth until it filled it and was coursing down
his neck and chest. He could feel Stone eyeing him,
but he took his time; a man couldn't sort out his
thoughts about a thing like that in a hurry.

"Well?" Stone said. Stone's voice was still hostile
and belligerent. "I heard the shootin'; sounded like
they all come at once."

Alec corked the bottle and hung it on the saddle

pommel. "They did." he said. "They come in a crowd; they had a trooper leadin' 'em—like I thought they might have. Just a kid, Stone. Not even as old as Pike."

"A trooper! A sure-enough Blue Ned?"

"A trooper," Alec said. "A sergeant-trooper; even got close enough for me to see his stripes."

"Gawdalmighty," Stone marveled. "I sure wish I'd been there. Damn it, Alec! You had your nerve stickin' that gun on me!"

Alec wasn't listening; he was seeing it all again—the proud and futile charge across the slope, the white spotted horse plunging and twisting and falling, the smooth, clean face of the dead boy in the moonlight. It was stuck in his head and wouldn't go.

"That broke it up," Alec said. "When he went down it took the heart out of the rest of 'em; they swung and scattered. I could 'a spent the rest of the night there if I'd cared to."

"Yellow-bellies," Stone scoffed. "Damn nesters ain't got no guts nohow. I always said they didn't. Got their nerve comin' out here and spoilin' the country for the rest of us. They won't last, though, damn it."

They were going forward again, slanting through the foothills toward the Guadeloupes, and Alec took his hat off and pushed his fingers through the bullet hole in the crown.

"Yes, they will, Stone," he said after a minute. "They ain't got the way of things yet, that's all." Alec put the hat on and tugged at the brim to set it firmly on his head. "They're a little clumsy, and maybe unsure, but the day'll come when they can handle everything themselves; the day'll come when the government won't have to send no troopers out here anymore. By God, Stone, New Mexico might even get to be a state some day."

Stone said "Ha!" and then he was quiet.

They kept to the high ground and slowly worked their way toward the top of the ridge and the Guadeloupes. It was hard, steep going; the horses stumbled blindly from fatigue and the two men jogged wearily with the yawning motion. They were silent for a great while.

Stone rode slumped forward, the pain in his arm bunching him tight, but Alec, now and then, would look around. Up high like they were he could see a good deal of country to the east, falling down the slope toward the Pecos and the valley. It was mostly-grey-yellow with sharp black gashes where the sun scratched a shadow, but over near the river a soft new green was coming with the spring—delicate and tentative, spreading along the acequias and the Pecos bed. There seemed to be a good deal more of that than in any year before, and the implications made Alec shake his head with a slow, sad wonder.

Going higher, the coarse outcroppings of rock and ragged brush growth gave way at last to the vanguard of the pine and cedar, the beginning of the timber being mostly stunted and undernourished, the roots clutching voraciously at the thin topsoil in their will to live. Beyond a ways, and higher still, the soil lay thicker underfoot, and the humus caused the timber growth to rise full-bodied and thick-boled, these trees lifting cool and green, enriching the air with their scent and moisture. Shy birds batted back and forth along the branches, the small ground creatures scurried audibly about the forest carpet; and one time, nearby a coyote barked.

"Goin' to rain." Stone made his first utterance in many miles. "Sure as hell goin' to rain when a coyote yaps after sun-up."

"Bound to some day," Alec agreed, "but not this one. Leastwise, it ain't goin' to rain on the say-so of *that* coyote."

Stone half-turned to look at him. "It ain't, huh?

How come you're so sure about this here particular coyote?"

Alec was smiling; it was fun to play with Stone. "Well, I figure I know this particular coyote pretty well. I figure I just about know the limits of his talents; and bringin' rain ain't among 'em."

Stone's eyes peered out sharply from beneath their ledges, and his lower lip came forward. "It ain't, huh?"

"Furthermore," Alec said, "it's my bet this coyote ain't no regular kind of coyote. He's a two-legged one that walks around on his hind feet just like you and me." Alec rose up on his stirrups and squinted through the thinning trees. " 'S matter of fact, Stone, he's right over there."

Stone swerved around, one hand half-dropping for his gun; then he relaxed and swore. "Isidro," he said. "Damn your Spanish eyes."

They came into the temporary camp, dismounted, removed their saddles and blankets and flopped on the ground. Alec had never been so tired in his life. All night long he'd been either riding or lying on his belly in the rocks; but that was only part of it. That part of the weariness would go away; a snooze would fix that. It was the killing of the boy-trooper that wouldn't lift. Maybe never.

He was hungry and he ate the cold fawn-meat and the corn bread the Apache brought, but the others wouldn't let him sleep when he was finished with the food. He had to tell them how it went.

"Very faintly we could hear it," Isidro said. "Pop, pop, pop, way, far away."

"We holed up in the Black," Alec explained. "There wasn't much shootin' before that. Some, but not much. We figured to stall 'em there, maybe scare 'em off without a fight. Hell, we couldn't keep ridin' forever, and they was stickin' with us pretty good by the time the moon come out."

"I think that is what we hear, then," Isidro said. "We hear it all at once, but very far away. Were there many?"

"Ten maybe; they spread out after a while and it was hard to tell."

Clint and Roy edged in closer and Clint grinned up at Stone.

"How many was left when it was finished, Stone?"

Stone hesitated, his eyes on Alec. "I ain't sure," he said. "Better ask Alec; I wasn't around when that happened."

Clint's mouth was slightly open and the ridge of his nose was shining. "Wasn't there? Why, Alec just now said you had a scrap . . . and we heard the shootin'."

"Stone wasn't there," Alec put in quick, "because he'd been already hit in the first of it, and I sent him to the other side of the Black; before it was over."

Clint's eyes flickered back and forth from Alec to Stone, slow meaning coming into them. Then Stone swung around and blazed at Alec.

"He put his damn gun on me, that's what he did! I no sooner git this nick than he put his gun on me and prodded me on my horse, shootin' at me even! I wasn't even lookin' at him!"

Alec tried to keep his voice down. "That's ain't so, Stone. I didn't know how long we could hold on there. I figured to get you out before you really had to run for it and maybe get killed 'cause you couldn't get away or stay on your horse."

"You done it 'cause you think you're God hisself," Stone said. "You done it 'cause you wanted to come up here and stick your thumbs in your unwashed armpits and have everyone bow and scrape at your feet."

Alec stood up abruptly. He'd never gone this far

with Stone before and he felt his control slipping out of his body. He hadn't asked for this, but, by God, Stone had.

"Listen, Stone," he said. "Listen carefully if you can. What you think of me don't make a big enough hill of sand to plant Indian corn in, but what you think of these others does. It weren't our purpose to lay there in the Black 'till we was shot so full of holes we'd 'a filled with water and sunk. It was our purpose to draw that posse off and then get back to the bunch—alive and whole. And we done it. Luckily, when you went up the bank they heard that noise and they quit tryin' to surround us, like they damn near did. They quit and they come right out in a bunch, thinkin' no doubt that we was runnin' off. They was in the open, then, and it weren't so hard."

When Alec stopped talking, Isidro's lips were smiling softly and Clint's eyes were as big as a pair of newly-minted silver dollars. Stone's face had turned the color of pine ashes; Stone's face looked like it'd never had a drop of blood in it at all.

Alec spoke into the big silence, saying, "I wasn't thinkin' particularly about drawin' 'em out by sendin' you away, but that's what happened, so I reckon it served a couple purposes. That don't make no never-mind now, though. The important thing about it is that them nesters had a trooper leadin' 'em; and he's dead. I killed him."

"Oh-ho," Isidro said quietly. "A trooper. Mmmm."

"That's why they come up here at night, then," Pike said.

Clint's eyes, still big and round, were filling with an awareness of the complication. "It ain't just nesters around here, is it, then? Must be more troopers where that one come from."

"That's what I'm gettin' at," Alec said, and curiously, he was glad that it was Clint who'd made the observation. "I think we got to get on out. The Territory's gettin' more troopers every day; they're set to make the law stick. We ain't goin' to have such easy livin' any more. That scrap last night was only a taste of it. Ask the Apache how it is to fight 'em regular."

The renegade had come up during the first of the talk and he was sitting cross-legged on the ground. When Alec turned to him the dark face was expressionless and non-commital, and only his black eyes showed an understanding of what was said.

"Them troopers are tough customers, ain't they?" Alec said.

The Apache nodded slowly. "Bad. Bad medicine. Heap bad. No damn good."

"There y'are," Alec said. "From a man who's fit 'em before. They ain't nothin' to play with. Where there's one there's more, and they'll be comin' up here now."

"Hell they will," Stone said. "They ain't enough of 'em yet. Them nesters only had one and they ain't got him no more."

"They'll get 'em, though," Alec argued. "That kind of news travels fast these days. They're comin', I tell you; and it won't do for us to wait for 'em. I'm thinkin' we ought to head on out—maybe go across to Arizona. They say Bisbee and Tombstone's pretty good towns; the people out there ain't so likely to shy off when we walk down the street."

Pike was leaning back on his elbows, his face upturned toward the sky above the forest. "Kind of bald out there, I hear," he said quietly. "Ain't many trees, except in the mountain country; ain't much out there but desert and them minin' towns."

"And who the devil wants to live in a damn town?" Roy said. "A man can't even turn around in them things, let alone live like he ought to."

Stone's knees were bent up beneath his chin and he was staring through the trees. "Nesters. Nothin' but nesters down there. They ain't goin' to move me out 'o here; they ain't goin' to trot me over there to Arizona, or no other place, if'n I ain't a mind to go."

Stone raised his head and looked at Clint. "What about you, Clint? You set to be run off the land you was born to?"

Clint hitched at his belt before he said anything. Clint had been emulating Stone for so long it was surprising to Alec that he had an opinion of his own.

"Well, I sure ain't set to run off to Arizona, Stone. It wouldn't pleasure me none to live in them minin' towns at all. But"—Clint's hand strayed up and explored the bandage on his head—"maybe we could just move on north a bit, say a hundred miles or so. The troopers might not look that far, and the nesters 'round here wouldn't have no interest in us once we was gone."

Clint looked hopefully at Stone.

The group was quiet while the men turned the new thought over in their heads. Alec let his eyes slide around the ring of faces, and he saw a tentative approval in most of them, except for Stone. He didn't think it was such a good idea, himself, not enough distance—but it was a start, and he could maybe talk them into Arizona later.

"Don't sound too bad." Roy was the first to speak. "Just so I don't have to go over there in that desert."

"Pike," Alec said, "what's your say?"

Pike looked carefully at Alec before he answered. "Might be we could give it a try. Things ought to be all right up there a bit, providin' we was careful."

"Isidro?"

Isidro shrugged. "Quién sabe? We go here, we go there; in time it is all the same, no matter what place. But, I go."

Alec smiled to himself as Isidro turned the brim of his hat in his fingers. Of all of them, only Isidro, with his native intuition, could see beyond their immediate situation. Only Isidro, and maybe Pike, in his groping, boyish way. But the others were all lost and they didn't know it.

"What about you?" Alec said to the Apache, and the Apache nodded vigorously. He didn't have to go beyond that, or elaborate, and Alec knew the renegade's memory of the Arizona fighting with Geronimo was very green and real.

Then Stone picked up a cedar branch and heaved it across the clearing with his good arm. "I don't like bein' shoved," he said with sullenness. "I don't like them nesters to think they got the best 'o me. This here land's free and open and I can walk on it if'n I choose."

"Them people down there don't even know who you are," Alec said quietly. "Which is a blame good thing to my way of thinkin'."

"Yeah? Well, I do. And I know I'm bein' shoved." Stone glared at the ground in front of him.

Alec felt again that he was talking to a small and willful child; Stone's stubbornness, in the face of the odds and dangers, made him marvel that the thick-faced man had lived as long as he had.

"Look, Stone," Alec said. "We're just goin' up here a little bit. Not far; we ain't goin' all the way to Arizona. We're only goin' up here and rest and breathe easy for awhile. We got some men here that's hurt—yourself is one—and we can't be takin' on the army. We got to get back in shape."

After the long quiet Stone finally looked at Alec. "All right, then," he said. "I don't favor it, but I'll go. But them damn nesters and homesteaders are goin' to pay for this. They ain't goin' to forget they shoved Stone Johnson off his range."

• CHAPTER 5 •

"I Used to Know a Girl . . ."

INSIDE THE BUILDING IT WAS QUIET AND MUSTY-SMELLING and Alec could see the small dust hanging in the sun-shaft at the window. Through the open door, the street-sounds were near and close, and standing at the counter, half-turned, he could see the horses plodding through the dust, the wagon and rigs and carts and traps creaking and jogging past, and the men and women jamming the board walks on either side of the dirt-choked road. The people he could see were of all conditions and dressed in all manner of clothing, from buckskin leggings and moccasins to pink ruffled parasols brought on from the East—though he paid no particular attention to any of them. It was simply his impression that there were way too many people in that place and that it was a marvel they could all get into it without there bein' a riot every minute or so. There was a brash impa-tience about everything there that made him feel unsettled and ill at ease. It made him feel the way that Roy had felt about the towns in Arizona.

Alec turned his head and pushed his hand into the pocket of his trousers when the man in the canvas apron licked his pencil stub and added up the tally.

"I guess that's about all we need just now," Alec said.

The storekeeper was a florid-faced man whose nose was beading in sweat and whose smile was ingratiating.

"You don't want to make up your mind about that too fast, now, you gentlemen," he said. "Gents of your appearance likely need more than flour and bacon and coffee."

"I don't reckon we are," Alec said. "What do you say, Pike? Isidro?"

"Well, maybe you ought to have somethin' you ain't yet seen," the storekeeper said. "I got things to sell that ain't on the shelves. Maybe you gents is aimin' to settle in these parts; maybe you're lookin' for a piece of bottom land or two."

"I don't reckon we are," Alec said. "Just passin' through."

The storekeeper did not seem to hear what Alec said. "Now, I got a few acres just out of town, here, a mile or so south—on the Carlsbad road; right on the river. Best damn growin' land in the Territory. Just been waitin' for the right lookin' man to come along."

"Maybe you didn't hear what I said," Alec said.

The storekeeper's smile was expansive. "Oh, sure, I heard, all right; I just figured you might be changin' your mind. Like as not you gents are headin' out to one of the ranches hereabouts."

The storekeeper's eyebrows made a question out of it and Alec shifted on his feet. He jerked his head with meaning at the pile of stores on the counter as Pike and Isidro came up to look at them.

"Looks like everything to me," Pike said. "Can't think of nothin' else. Got tobaccy? Can't do without that." Pike's eyes began to wander around the shelves behind the counter.

"We got tobaccy," Alec said. "I reckon that's all, then."

"Maybe I ought to have one o' them pipes up there in that bowl," Pike said, pointing. "One of them cob ones."

Alec laughed. "What the devil you want one of them for, Pike? You can't smoke one while you're ridin'. Set your nose on fire. You'll likely sit on it and bust it anyhow."

The man in the canvas apron put the glass bowl of pipes on the counter and eyed Alec. "These here pipes are strong, mister. I don't figure a man could break one that way, less he was real stout. These come all the way from Missouri." The storekeeper cleared his throat. "Consigned to me by freight. I ordered 'em direct."

Pike pulled a fat one out of the bowl and put the bit in his mouth. Alec watched him out of the corner of his eye as he peeled the money for the tally off the roll of bills. "Seems I heard somewhere a pipe like that'd give a man consumption."

Pike removed the pipe from his mouth and looked at it carefully. The storekeeper lifted his glasses off his nose and commenced to polish them deliberately on a corner of the apron.

"Got your leg pulled, mister," he said. "Them there pipes is the best in the world; wouldn't have 'em if they weren't."

"No, don't suppose you would," Alec said. "Must'a been some other kind of pipe I heard about."

Pike put the pipe in his mouth again and chewed on the bit. "Feels all right to me, Alec. Don't see how a man could get consumption from a pipe like this one. Don't see how a man can get it out in this country nohow, with all this fine air."

The storekeeper put his glasses back on his nose and smiled. "Now, you said somethin', mister. This here air is the best there is in the world. I been livin' out here six months now, and I tell you there ain't nothin' like it. People comin' in every day; some comin' jest fer their health."

"Some leavin' it for the same reason, no doubt," Alec said, and the storekeeper eyed him again before going on.

"Well . . . I don't know much about that, there's sure a mess comin' in; and like I said, I got them fine river lots. A smart man'd buy 'em up before the price gets bid to the sky. This here Artesia's a fast growin' town."

Alec picked up the box the storekeeper had put everything in, and hefted it. "We're just passin' through," he said.

The storekeeper leaned on the counter with the fingers of his fat hands splayed on the wood. "Careful where you go around these parts," he said. "You gents don't want to go on down Carlsbad way 'less you don't favor your lives none. They had a big killin' down there the other day, a stage robbery, too, and them as did it fought a pitched battle in the hills that night. Killed near on to a dozen people; and some troopers, too. They figure there must'a been close to fifty in the gang."

"That sounds like quite a gang," Alec said.

"And they ain't been caught yet. Ain't likely to be long, though. They say the county's goin' to get the governor to send in a whole mess 'o troops."

"I reckon we ought to be careful, then," Alec said. "Pike. Isidro—let's go."

Going through the door, Alec heard the store-keeper calling to them. "Y'ought to think about them lots, gents. They ain't goin' to last."

"No, don't expect they will," Alec said.

They went on out to the tie-rail, swung up to saddle and rode on toward the outskirts of the town. Alec held the box balanced in front of him, moving it this way and that to avoid hitting the people with it in the close-packed streets. God, there was a crowd of 'em!

When the raw, new buildings began to give way to the run-down, mean adobe casas Pike took his pipe out of his mouth again and looked it over. "Alec," he said. "Alec, what'd you make that fuss about the pipe for? It sure looks all right to me."

"Oh, I don't know," Alec said after thinking on it for a moment. "I guess I just don't like to see them money grabbers have everything their own way. Don't seem right somehow."

"That one sell you the moon if you let him," Isidro said.

Pike looked at him. "The moon? Nobody owns that, Isidro."

Isidro laughed quietly and looked around. "That is nothing," he said. "He would try. He would try to sell you anything."

Just beyond the outskirts of the town they crossed the new-built bridge over the acequia. A few yards further on a barbed-wire fence glistened in the morning sun, and they went parallel with this until they came upon a man guiding a plow behind a mule. His blue denim shirt was dark with sweat along his back and his black, home-spun pants were stuffed into flat-heeled clumsy boots, the soles of which were chunked with the new-turned earth. As they came near to him he dropped the reins over the handles of the plow and walked toward the fence, mopping at his bony-face with a red handkerchief.

"Howdy," the bony-faced man said. "You goin' to be neighbors?"

"Reckon not," Alec said. "Don't know much about plowin'."

"Didn't know but what you was. Feller come by earlier—goin' to be over there a bit from me. Lots of 'em comin' in now."

The man's voice had a flat twang to it—something like the storekeeper's, Alec thought—and he said, "You come out here from the east? From Missouri maybe?"

The nester smiled and scraped his boot on the middle strand of wire. "More or less east. Came from Indiana—name of Harris."

Pike leaned slightly forward in his saddle, squinting off across the field of new furrows. "What you goin' to grow in there, mister?"

"Alfalfa. Goin' to grow alfalfa in there; I wish I could'a got her down earlier, but I ain't been here but a couple weeks. Yes, sir, there's goin' to be a call for alfalfa, and I aim to be ready when I hear it."

"I reckon that fence ought to keep the alfalfa from runnin' off 'fore you're ready to sell it, then," Alec said.

The nester looked slowly at Alec and mopped his face again. "Ain't no alfalfa I know of can run off. That fence, there, that's to keep the cattle out; can't have no critters tramplin' 'round in there."

"They get the bloat if'n they eat green alfalfa, too," Pike said unexpectedly. "They get the bloat and they swell up big as a courthouse, and then die."

Alec looked at Pike. "Yeah? Where'd you hear that?"

Pike's young face colored when he smiled. "Reckon I knowed that for quite awhile, Alec. Learned it long ago; just kept it in my head, I guess."

"Ho, he is like a farmer himself," Isidro said, and Pike's color got even deeper.

After they left the barbed-wire they went for nearly an hour across the flats before the land began to lift again. Once beyond the fertility of the river and the acequias the earth commenced to parch and grey again; the soil harden from the lack of moisture, and the vegetation to surrender to invasion of the hardy desert plants. Climbing into the foothills, they paused before entering a patch of dwarf pine, and looked back across the valley.

"Kind of pretty down there, ain't it?" Pike said. "I don't mean all them people, or nothin' like that. I mean the way them nesters are makin' good soil with them ditches—turnin' the river in like that."

"Sí," Isidro said. "It is very nice; it is like life."

Alec stared hard at the valley and tried to appreciate it in the way that Pike and Isidro did, but he couldn't. It wasn't an easy thing for him to do any more; he'd been away from it too long. Isidro and Pike were different because Pike was young and had been a rancher not too very long ago, and Isidro'd come from the soil just like any plant growing out there in the valley; men like Isidro never really left it. But Alec—Alec could only try to get the feel of what they meant.

Pike was still gazing toward the Pecos, his hat tipped back, leaving a red ring on his forehead, when he spoke to Alec. Alec was looking hard at him and the slow curve of Pike's lips remained in his head.

"Alec," Pike said. "Alec—the bunch's 'bout done, ain't it? The way that Stone went crazy at the stage and brought them vigilantes on us like that is goin' to be the end, ain't it?"

Alec thought carefully before he answered. "It could be," he said in a moment. "It could be the end; my killin' that trooper's the beginnin' of it, I figure." Alec had to force himself to speak about the trooper; directly in the forefront of his mind he saw the dark, reaching arm with the chevrons creasing the sleeve and the saber outthrust.

Isidro edged his horse nearer to Alec and looked at him intently. "Alec, amigo—Alec, you should not curse inside because of that. The fault does not lie with you, but with Stone."

"I pulled the trigger," Alec said.

"It is Stone's fault, from the beginning. Maybe you should have let him take his chances when he was hurt, instead of sending him off and fighting alone."

"Well, I didn't," Alec said. Why hadn't he, he wondered or, why hadn't he ridden out with Stone and let the cards fall where they would? Alec shooed a fly out of the horse's mane. "I killed him, Isidro, and that's all there is to it."

"It's still the end, though, ain't it?" Pike said again. Pike was looking directly at Alec and his nostrils were flared slightly. "Just a matter of time, I mean."

"I reckon it's here to stay," Alec said. "What's on your mind?" he asked, but he already knew; and he felt he was glad because of it.

Now Pike pulled off his hat, smashed it with his balled fist and stared at the sweat and hair grease that soiled the inside of the crown. "I guess I don't really know how to say it now that I come to it," he said. "I had it all figured out in my head, but now it won't come straight." Pike smashed the hat viciously and pulled it back on his head.

"I know what it is," Alec said; Alec's voice was kind, like that of a father about to gratify the wish of his son. "You want to leave, don't you, Pike? Seein' the changes come over this valley got into you, no? Got to pullin' at them old ties."

"I reckon it's here to stay," Pike said quietly. "I'm happy up there in the hills; I'm happy when we're ridin' footloose and free as the air, livin' like we don't owe nothin' to no one, steppin' where we please without a 'scuse-me or a thank-you." Pike turned his eyes into the valley again; his body was humped in the saddle and his fingers were twisting the reins.

"But I got the smell of that land down there, Alec. I got a look at plowed ground again and a look at them cabins down there in the lowlands. If'n you won't bear me no grudge, Alec, I'd like to go on back to the Cristos ... I'd get me some land up there, or some cattle ... and, well ... I used to know a girl ..."

Alec had it all thought out before he answered. It came quick to his tongue and he knew he must have had the answer a great while back. He was glad to see Pike go ... yes, happy about it.

"I think it's a fine thing, Pike. It's good. The sooner you start out the better."

"I figure I'd go back to camp with you and take my leave of the rest. They maybe ain't the best in the world, but we was together."

"Don't know if I'd do that if I was you," Alec said. "Stone ain't likely to understand about your goin'."

Pike adjusted his hat. "I ain't afraid of Stone."

"I know you ain't," Alec said. "But there ain't no need to get him riled and maybe settin' somethin' off." Alec laughed and made a pass at Pike's arm with his fist. "Think 'o me, Pike! I'm goin' to have a hard enough time keepin' the peace, without you bein' there to aggravate the situation more. You better just take off now."

"He is right," Isidro said to Pike. "Sí, yes—that Stone, he will be bad. You make it more easy to go now."

Pike looked off toward the north, along the trail he would follow to the Cristos. "Come to think of it, why'nt you two come with me? Like you say, it's about done; sure ain't too soon to be settlin' down."

Alec poked one foot deeper into its stirrup. "Sure sounds good," he said. "But I reckon I'll stick it out until there ain't no one left but me."

"I stay with Alec," Isidro said simply. "Of course, he is a fool to remain, but some day we may come."

"Well, I'll be lookin' for you," Pike said. Pike moved his horse off a dozen paces or so, then looked back. "Well, so long."

"So long, Pike," Alec said.

"Adios, amigo." Isidro removed his hat and fluttered it above his head.

Pike smiled his quick, boy's smile, flipped his hand at them, and wheeled his horse toward the north. He did not look around again.

The dust was lying flat again when Alec and Isidro resumed the trail. Pike was a far dot along the ground and Alec had ceased to look at him; he had an emptiness inside him and watching after Pike seemed to make it more acute.

"You should have gone with him." Isidro said roughly. "It is like he said. We are done. We could be happy in the mountains. They are very beautiful, the Cristos."

"I wasn't speakin' for you," Alec said. "You could have gone. Why in hell didn't you?"

Isidro shrugged. "Quién sabe? Who knows why not? Maybe I with you too long. Yes, that must be it. It would be so easy if I never see you at all."

• CHAPTER 6 •
Four Against Two

GOING ON INTO THE HILLS, THE QUESTION KEPT POPPING into Alec's head; it tended to open up a whole new avenue of self-inquiry. Why hadn't he gone? Yes, just why the devil hadn't he and Isidro turned off there with Pike and gone on up to the Cristos?

What do you owe to Stone and Clint and Roy and the Apache, anyway? his mind asked him. What do you owe to them that you've got to stay on there with 'em, watchin' over 'em and waitin' for the end, which is sure to come? Alec, you ain't got no sense nohow. Alec, you ain't got the sense you was born with.

How come you think you're so high and mighty, Alec? You think you're God, or something? What makes you think you can calm Stone down; what makes you think you can keep the others—Roy and Clint—from gettin' to be spittin' murderous images of Stone? Is that why you're sittin' it out like this? You think there's maybe a chance for 'em even if there ain't one for Stone no more? A fine one you are to tell *them* what to do; how to live—you that killed a trooper.

Killed a trooper, didn't you? Kind of a turning point for you, ain't it, Alec? You never did a killin' like that before; you never fought the law in just that way, did you? Come to think of it, there wasn't much law of any kind around these parts 'till recently, was there? A man more or less held the law in his own hands; especially with that Tunstall business, that got the Lincoln war agoin'. A man just chose the side that seemed to represent his interests, and the right as he saw it.

Up until the trooper, then, there was some hope for you, wasn't there? Not so much now, though. Lots of fellers took the wrong road out of the cattle war. Lots of fellers took to robbin' a stage now and then, maybe takin' some beef when they was hungry, and yes, maybe shootin' things up on occasion—perhaps a killin' when they was up against it and had no choice.

There was nothin' so awful wrong with that, now; there was nothin' wrong with that, and a body was still a true man and honest 'cause he was only doin' what everyone else was and it was the way of life in this country, it was that way 'cause youngsters like you did their growin' up durin' the cattle fracas and didn't know any different; there was no one to teach you any different. They simply stuck a gun in your hand when you was sixteen and said, "We got to fight fer our livelihood, kid; see you use that iron right." And so for ten long years you did all that they told you to, and when it was over you'd gained nothin' but a big bewilderment about everything—and a liking for living free and wild.

There was some hope for you up until the trooper, though. You could have pulled out of the whole she-bang with a clear conscience, but the trooper changed it all. He was probably a pretty nice young kid—just like you used to be, just doin' what he was told. And you had it in your power to let him live. You could have just rid on out of the Black, there, when Stone got hurt, and kept goin'—lettin' Stone take his chances on makin' it back to the Guadeloupes.

But, no; no, you had to send Stone on his way and be big and noble about the whole business. You had to stay there and fight a rear-guard action, and you had to kill the trooper. And you know what you done when you done that, don't you? That was the government you killed, Alec. That was the government, all right, and you didn't mean to do that, now, did you?

Like it or not, Alec, the government represents the same things you was fightin' for in the Lincoln war; the right of a man to go where he pleases and do what he likes, unmolested. To make his livin' as he sees fit to. Your thinkin' muddled on that? It means them nesters and homesteaders back there in the valley—even that a nickel-nursin' storekeeper—got a right to be there, just like you got a right to be where you are. And they're fightin' for their end of justice just like you was fightin' for yours in the Lincoln scrap; only they're better off than you was 'cause they got the troopers out here now, when there wasn't much like that before.

You think Stone was worth that? You think Stone would ever do that for you? You think, if he ever had any principles—which he ain't, of course—that he'd compromise 'em for you? He'd do a killin', all right, 'cause there ain't nothin' he'd rather do, but he sure wouldn't stay in a hole to help you out of one. So it all comes back to this peculiar sense of loyalty you got, Alec. It sure made a mess 'o your life, ain't it; and it looks like it's goin' to keep it up. You're goin' to pay for killin' that trooper, Alec. You're goin' to pay for killin' that trooper. It don't make no difference that Stone's slaughter at the stage got it all agoin'; the trooper was your business, and you're goin' to do the payin' there—with anguish, and self-damnation, and maybe in the end, blood.

"Damn it," Alec said aloud. "Damn it, damn it to hell."

"Alec. Alec, what are you saying?" It was Isidro, turned in his saddle and looking at him.

Alec became slowly conscious of Isidro, of riding the horse, the box across the saddle in front of him, and of the high trees to all sides. They had come into the deep timber again, and his sweat-soaked body was suddenly chilled in the shade. He wiped his face with his free hand and smiled self-consciously.

"Can't for a fact think what I was sayin'."

"You say, 'damn it,'" Isidro said. "You say it several times. What is in your head?"

"Oh . . . I don't know, Isidro. Don't make no difference what it was anyway." Alec looked beyond Isidro, into the tangle of brush and the deep vistas in the aisles of the trees. His mind had been wandering for quite a long time. They were nearly into the temporary camp; he could smell the faint smoke from the Apache's fire, and in another moment he could hear the snorting of the horses in their hobbles. "I'll tell you some time," Alec added. "No time now; we're here."

Stone and Clint and Roy stood around them in a semi-circle while they got down from their horses. The Apache took the box and carried it to the fire, but the others remained where they were and Alec could tell that something had got into them. At first, he thought it was going to be about the missing Pike, but when Stone hitched at his belt and commenced to talk he knew it wasn't.

"How was it down there, Alec?"

"Artesia? Hot. Hot and dusty, and filled up to the seams."

"I don't mean that. I mean how was they talkin'? What was they sayin' about the ruckus the other night?"

Alec slipped his cinches and hoisted the saddle and blanket off his horse before he answered. "They got a blowed up story about it," he said then. "They got a yarn up from Carlsbad sayin' we had fifty men and that we killed nigh on to a dozen. The story grows with every mile it travels."

Stone made a circle in the earth with the toe of his boot. "When was you plannin' on leavin' here?" he asked.

"I figure the sooner the better," Alec said. "Ain't no sense in stayin' in these parts any longer than need be. We got the food now, so we better get on with it. There's some talk down there about gettin' Wallace to send in some troopers."

Stone squatted on his heels and poked at the ground with a pine branch. "We been thinkin' some," he said. "While you was gone we been thinkin' things over and we decided them nesters down there ought to have somethin' to remember us by." Stone looked up and grinned.

"You did, huh," Alec said. "Just like that."

"Just like that," Stone said. Stone was still grinning.

Alec looked over Stone's head at Clint and Roy, and at the Apache who was sidling up beside them. "Is he speakin' for you, too? Ain't you got no tongues of your own?"

Clint flushed and bulged his lower lip out. "I guess I done my own thinkin' all right; Stone's just speakin' for us, that's all."

"That's right," Roy said. Roy spaced his feet wide and rested his hands on his hips. Beside him, the Apache nodded.

Alec took his hat off, wiped at his forehead with the back of his hand, and put the hat on again. "Ain't you got no sense? You know what you're gettin' into? You goin' to let Stone get you massacred? That valley's on fire. We can maybe get out now, but if you pull some fool trick down there they'll hunt you into the deepest hole this country's got."

Stone flipped the stick into the brush and stood up. "We took a vote on it," he said. "We got to thinkin' you give up too easy, Alec. We figured it ain't right for us to be pushed around and we aim to let them that's doin' it have a remembrance of who they was pushin'. So, we voted to go down there tonight and let some one of 'em have it. We figured you ought to have a say in it, too, so now we're askin', do you want to come?"

"I don't want no part of it," Alec said. "You can't go takin' after people that way. It ain't right to bother 'em like that."

Isidro polished one of the conches on his belt with the sleeve of his shirt. "I do not want a part in that either," he said.

"Countin' the vote again, that looks like four against two." Stone looked around and his smile went away. "Where's Pike?"

Alec felt his hand drifting toward his belt. "He's gone."

"Gone?" Stone said. It was very still in the clearing. "What d'you mean, gone? Gone where?"

"Just gone," Alec said. "He's smart, Stone. He's smarter'n you or me, or the whole bunch of us put together. He knew when to quit."

"You let him quit?" Stone's face was wide and vacant, as though he wasn't sure just what it was he was listening to. It was so still now that Alec could hear the faint breeze in the highest crowns of the trees.

"I even told him to go," Alec said. Alec was watching Stone hard and he felt the tension coming into everyone. It was another one of those times when Stone was weighing the odds, and peering into Stone's far-back eyes, Alec could almost get a glimpse of his thought process. He knew that Stone could maybe count on himself and perhaps Clint, but that Roy and the Apache might not be worth the gamble and that a lot of blood would be spilled before anything was settled. Slowly, Stone relaxed and smiled.

"Well . . . well, I guess that's it, then, ain't it boys? I just reckon Alec don't care if this bunch sticks together anymore or not. I reckon he don't have the right to tell us what to do now, does he? I guess it don't make much difference if he comes with us or not."

"I guess it don't, Stone," Alec said. "I reckon it's your outfit now."

• CHAPTER 7 •
Fire

"CARAMBA!" ISIDRO SAID. "IT IS DARK LIKE THE BEAR I
tell you of one time."

Alec drew his horse in and turned his head. "Not
so blamed loud, Isidro. What bear you talkin'
about?"

"The bear with the belly," Isidro said. "It is dark
like the one with the belly. I can just see my hand in
front of my face!"

"Them clouds make it that way," Alec said. "A
good thing, too. We can get a devil of a lot closer
without them stars shinin' on us; and that late
moon."

"Can you tell where they are?" Isidro said after a
few paces. "I have seen nothing since night fell."

"Ain't got much more than an idea," Alec said. "I
just figure they'll lead us to the nearest nesters."

"Do you think they know we follow them?" Isidro
said. "The Apache may have his ear on the ground;

he is like an animal with that ear. I think he can hear the world turning with it."

"I don't think they're takin' any time to do that; anyway, Stone's got the idea we don't want to be anywhere near his doin's."

"We do not, do we?" Isidro said. "Is he not right?"

Alec grinned into the darkness. "I reckon he's right, all right; lots of places I'd rather be, but I figure this is the place I ought to be. If we can just toss in some confusion that'll be enough."

"Then we go away, Alec. We then go far away, do we not?"

"Yeah," Alec said. "We'll go far, far away, Isidro."

"Did you observe the Apache?" Isidro said in a little while. "Bow, arrows, knife, his hair in braids and smeared with grease. He should not be with them, should he?"

"No," Alec said. "He shouldn't, but he is. I reckon he stayed with Stone 'cause Stone said he'd take him out for blood. He'd never go out with me, though; go crazy like a wolf."

"What good is that bow in the dark?" Isidro said. "What can he hope to hit with that when he cannot even see how he is holding it?"

"I don't know; maybe just to make him feel big."

"I think the French wine make him feel big, too," Isidro said. "I think it make him feel just like Geronimo." Isidro paused and then spoke rapidly, and with wonder. "Alec . . . look; look over there, that star. It is a comet!"

Alec looked up quickly and saw the bright streak arcing across the sky. It seemed very near; it was much too near to be a comet. When it struck a slow flame spread away from it, and presently another one fled across the blackness and a new patch of flame flowed away from it. This time it gave sufficient light for Alec to see the cabin and outbuildings.

"Ain't no comets, Isidro," he said. "Them's arrows. Reckon the renegade can see pretty well after all.''

With the first of the arrows they had reined in to watch them strike; and now in the deep quiet of the land the high yell came toward them from the nester's ground. It was such a yell that made Alec sit up ramrod straight and cause his blood to take a sudden chill. He had not heard one like that for nearly twenty years and the remembrance of the wagon train was in his head again. He would never forget the way the attackers whooped when circling in.

The fire spread rapidly, for the roof of the cabin was dry, and it burned well. The light from it flowed like water across the ground, flooding the dark with illumination, and as he moved in closer with Isidro, Alec could presently see the shadowed figures riding their horses through the outer perimeter of the light. Nearer in, someone who appeared to be the Apache was crouching close to a shed, and as he swung his bow around the corner, one of the cabin casements opened and the image of a man aimed a rifle into the night. Coincidental with his firing, the arrow left the Apache's bow; the rifle fell, and the man stumbled backward with the arrow setting his shirt on fire.

Alec and Isidro were nearly a hundred yards away when they dismounted and Alec saw the arrow go through the window. It was surprising that he could pick out such detail at that distance, even though the fire was very bright and spreading rapidly. Perhaps he had only imagined the renegade near the outbuildings, but the arrow had come straight from it and there had been no mental trickery in the nester's falling back with the arrow blazing in his face.

The yelling was very plain as they hung low to the ground and went forward afoot. All four of the raiders were now circling the buildings on their horses, just out of reach of the clear light. Sometimes one of them could be seen as a vague, dim shape, going past the flames, but mostly Alec had to depend on their gun-streaks to determine their location.

Now that the surprise was over there was shooting from the cabin, too. All the casements Alec could see were open, and from each there came a sporadic but continuing fire. It gave him an idea of the number of defenders, and it presently occurred to him, with pleasure, that the raid might well entail more effort than Stone had realized. Still, there was the fire, and with a house like that one it was only a matter of time before the roof fell in.

Nearer still, Alec could see the details of the construction and he could appreciate Stone's selection of that particular one. A good many of the houses and casas going up around there were of adobe mud, but Stone had found one built of timber, patched here and there with rude planks, and covered with a pitched roof of hand-split shingles.

At a point less than two hundred feet from the buildings, Alec and Isidro slipped into a shallow draw. They were very close to everything in there; the details of everything were quite plain to see, and now the sound of the fire, which Alec had not been able to clearly hear in the beginning, passed in a low consuming roar around them. A moderate breeze was coming into the valley from the Guadeloupes, and unhindered by any obstacles, was sweeping the shredded flames along the roof of the cabin.

"Madre de Dios!" Isidro hissed. "That is an inferno! How can they live in there?"

"Folks can stand a lot if'n they have to," Alec said. "But I don't reckon they can put up with that much longer."

"It makes one sick to watch," Isidro said. "We are bad, you and I, Alec, but we are never bad like this. To burn a man's house!"

"It's goin' to get worse, I think. It's only the beginnin'. If they was only goin' to set it afire their job's done. But they're still ridin' around out there.''

Isidro spoke in an awed voice. "You think they wait for them to come out? You think they wait to kill them all?"

"I think so," Alec said, and he was astonished that the acceptance of the idea came so easily. But they were; they were going to do it. They were going to keep circling around that place until the nesters were smoked out, and that would bring the end.

Nothing they had ever done was like this, Alec was thinking. Nothing—the killings at the stage, or any other of the depredations that had occurred in the past—came up to this. Perhaps the thought of this had been in his head before it all began—early in the evening, when Stone and Clint and Roy were drinking the remainder of the champagne and swaggering around with shiny, mean faces, and when the Apache was fingering the treasures in his war bundle and getting ready for the warpath he'd left so long ago. Perhaps the inevitability of this climax in their actions had been in his head and explained his easy acceptance of it now.

But it was insane and macabre, and in a sense beyond his comprehension. He had brought Isidro down from the hills, following the others, under the vague compulsion of breaking up whatever deviltry Stone might lead them into, but there was no breaking up a thing like this. There was no way to extinguish the fire in that house, or worse, to quench the blood-lust of the hellions which were following Stone's lead in his narrowing circles around the cabin.

Alec began to edge up out of the draw, one hand tugging at his gun. Isidro grabbed him from behind and held him.

"Alec! Amigo, have you lost your sense? Are you loco? What are you doing?" The whites of Isidro's eyes shone clearly in the light of the flames.

"I got to stop them somehow," Alec said. "I got to drive them out 'fore them people come out."

"Drive them away?" Isidro said. "Two of us against four? And what of those inside? They will shoot at us, too."

Alec was about to explain to Isidro that he didn't know how it was to be done, but that he was going to find a way, when a lull in the firing drew his eyes around to the cabin again. There was something missing beside the shooting, and in a moment he knew what it was; the sound of the running horses.

"They are on the other side of the cabin!" Isidro said. "They are waiting over there."

"I'll bet they're goin' to rush it," Alec said. "Must be a blind wall over there; that shootin' from this side likely got too much for 'em. Come on, we better get on with it."

"Wait. A moment, amigo." The peculiar, kindly note in Isidro's voice made Alec turn and stare at him. Isidro was smiling a gentle smile. It made him remember that Isidro was the closest friend he'd ever had. He had a great feeling for Isidro in that moment.

"What is it?"

"Do you know what we do?" Isidro said. "Do you know that we may die?"

"Yeah," Alec said. "I know, Isidro." Alec squinted into Isidro's bland face. "Isidro . . . you stay here. This ain't your business."

Isidro shrugged. "It may be, quién sabe? Do you do this because of the trooper? Is that in your mind, too?"

Alec thought it over. "Maybe. Part of it may be that."

"Then I go," Isidro said. "With you I go. It will be a pleasure."

Out of the draw, and edging forward on his belly, Alec was conscious of their nakedness. There was brush and loose rock and stunted clumps of vegetation all around them and between them and the cabin, but the fire played brightly upon all of it and made him feel that it was especially revealing for them. It did not make any difference that he was pressed into the gravel like a snake and that his face was plastered in the dirt, with his tongue and lips acquiring a thick paste of dust.

"How far do we go?" Isidro said patiently. Isidro was trying to make himself as thin as paper against the ground.

"As far as we can," Alec said. "If we can get back of them sheds maybe we can keep Stone and the others away from the house."

Isidro laughed with bravado. "A big hope, amigo."

"Maybe, but anyway, we try."

"Sí, we do that much," Isidro said.

They hunched forward a few more yards, then pressed flat as gunfire broke out, then died away again, beyond the cabin.

"From the inside, you think?" Isidro said.

"Can't tell," Alec said. "Dang fire's roarin' too hard."

Alec listened for it to come again and when he heard it that time it seemed to be coming from a place much farther from the cabin. It seemed to be coming from the direction of the river. Almost at once, then, he knew what it was.

"Posse comin'," he said to Isidro. "And it sure ain't surprisin' with all this fire lightin' up the country."

"I think we go now?" Isidro said.

"You go," Alec said. "I'll stay, for awhile anyway; they're still a ways off and Stone and them may try somethin' at the last minute."

"Alec, you come, it is too dangerous!"

"I'll come! I'll come! You go get the horses ready; you can edge 'em down this way if you care to. I won't be long here."

"I don't like this," Isidro said. "But I go; I bring them back. I bring them behind you."

"Not too damn close, now," Alec said. "That posse see 'em and they're finished."

"No, I be careful," Isidro said. Isidro patted Alec's back and commenced to edge away toward the draw again. Alec watched him slip into it, turning back toward the cabin again as the door opened and a man emerged.

He was better than a hundred feet away, but Alec knew he was on the point of suffocation from the smoke. He held a rifle in his hands, but the barrel was pointed aimlessly, hanging loosely as though the nester didn't know whether it was a gun or maybe a stick he was holding onto. He batted at his eyes with one hand, took a few shambling steps to the side and pitched over on the ground. At the same time, the doorway filled again as a woman and a pair of young ones made their way to the outside—and the Apache came slinking around the corner of the cabin.

Alec commenced to run. The sight of the renegade shot him to his feet and toward the cabin before the message of movement had recorded in his brain. He felt his rough stumbling and his boots pounding on the rock and gravel and the gun in his hand and the cabin was a thousand miles away and he thought he would never get there.

He saw the Apache, smooth-moving, his skin as sleek and shiny as that of a mountain cat, creeping toward the young ones and the woman, and his muscles bunching and his legs driving into a lope. He saw the woman turn an press her hands to her temples as though to keep her scream from forcing her brains out through her ears as the Apache hit her and she swung, her hair flying yellow in the light of the fire.

Alec was running like he had never run before. His breathing was tearing at his throat and lungs and yet for all his effort it seemed that what was happening to the woman was occurring in a place that he would never reach. Almost he made it. Almost he got to her in time; he was less than ten yards away when the Apache flung her to the ground, and he saw it all. He saw the woman lying on her belly, her arms outstretched, pushing up and her head arched back and her voice shrieking as the renegade twined the yellow hair in his hand and brought the knife down with the other. He saw the knife-point etch the small circle in the woman's skull and the blood bead out as the Apache wrenched the scalp away and swung it overhead.

Alec remembered the yellow scalp leaping out of the renegade's hand when he collided with him. He hit him with his whole body, bringing the gun barrel down in a blow at the Apache's head, and they rolled together on the ground. Pressed into each other, Alec caught the stench of the wine and the grease and the dead smell of the thick, rank hair and then they were apart again and the Apache was swinging the knife up from his knees. The blade caught Alec in the side, skidded on the ribs and sang high beyond his shoulder with the thrust. At the same time he brought the Colt around and fanned the hammer in a continuous roar and blaze of orange, and the renegade lifted with each shot and finally lay in a mess in front of him.

Alec got to his feet and heard the horses. He stood with the fog pressing into his head and with the numbness coming into his legs and body and he saw Isidro coming up and leading the other horse. All around there was gunfire now, and Isidro pulled at him frantically. Alec heaved on the pommel and cantle. He was conscious of his lack of strength and the fierce pain where the knife had cut him, but he kept on pulling and at last he was in the saddle. Then they were going forward in a surge, and as they passed a shed there was more shooting, but very near. In the flame's light, Alec saw Roy swing his rifle around as they went by, then turn and slide quietly against the timbers and he remembered that Isidro's aim had always been good from a moving horse.

• CHAPTER 8 •
The Last Time

ISIDRO CAME OUT OF THE ADOBE HOUSE AND WALKED across the small open space toward Alec, who was dozing in the sun just beyond the great cave of shade made by the lofty cottonwood. Alec heard him coming, but it was one of the luxuries of living up there in the Cristos that he did not have to be immediately on the alert whenever he heard footsteps. He took his time, and when Isidro sat on the ground beside him he opened first one eye and then the other; and he stretched widely and looked sleepily around him.

"We have something to eat soon," Isidro said to him. "Lupita, she fix something now, and soon we eat. Are you hungry?"

Alec yawned and opened both eyes together. "You blamed betcha, I'm hungry. What we havin'?"

"Oh, I think we have some frijoles, yes, we have some of those; perhaps some enchiladas." Isidro frowned and looked up into the cottonwood. "And some chicos? Yes, some of that, too, I think."

Alec laughed. "There'll be some o' that, all right. We ain't never goin' to run out o' corn."

Isidro regarded him reproachfully. "You don't like that, Alec? Chicos? I think Lupita is good with that. Of course, she is my wife for only a short time, and maybe she get better one day."

"It's all right," Alec said. "Best I ever tasted. I wasn't lookin' at it that way. I was just thinkin' it'd be nice to have a side of beef. Ain't had no beef in quite a while. Don't somehow seem right not to steal it anymore."

Isidro bent his knees up under his chin and looked at Alec solemnly. "We no longer steal the beef, Alec. And we have to wait for next year for ours. We have only a little stock now and they have to grow; yes, they must grow and have more. Soon, next year, perhaps, we have some to sell and some to eat, too."

"What d'you think of Pike's idea?" Alec said. "The other day, when he come up here visitin', he seemed to have a fair thought."

"Sí, it was a good one," Isidro said. "To put the two herds together would be fine. Do you like it?"

Alec rolled over on his belly and poked at the dirt with his finger. "Sounds good; sounds good as long as it's all right with him to bring his stuff up here. I don't like it too well where he is."

Isidro gazed at the mountains, raising magnificent and bold in the sun and sky. "I know," he said. "It is too near the road."

"It's smack on it," Alec said. "Ain't many can go to Santa Fe from the east without they go right by Pike's front door. I don't like all that activity."

"He likes the grass down there, but it is not bad here," Isidro said. "It is not even twenty miles to his place; I do not think he would mind to come here."

"Wouldn't take but a couple days to bring his stock up," Alec said. "We could get right at it. We could go down there next week and see about it."

"Sí, yes, if you feel well enough."

"I feel okay. Even the stiffness is gone."

Isidro raised his head and looked around them. Alec watched the expression on his face as the idea worked into his head and moved around. Isidro's eyes were always deep with light when he was concentrating on a thought.

"And we could build another casa here," he said after a moment. "We could build another for Pike—and you, Alec, if you no longer cared to live with us—and we would raise fine beef and be very happy."

Alec looked sidewise at Isidro. "I like it with you and Lupita; can't I live with you?"

"Como no! Of course, you can! Amigo, you can live with us until you fall over your beard! I only think that . . . well, who knows, perhaps we will raise more than beef, and the casa will be too small for so many."

Alec was still laughing when Lupita came to the door and called to them. The shadows from the peppers hanging on the roof beams made strange freckles upon her smooth, creamy face and upon the white blouse which covered the upper part of her body. Only the bright skirt and sturdy bare legs were caught in the full rays of the sun; though her teeth were white enough to be barely darkened by the shadows.

"Come, you two," she said. "We will eat, now; yes, we will eat, and you can make your great plans when we have finished."

Isidro turned lazily and smiled at her. "We come, muchacha; in a minute we will come."

"Now!" the round Lupita said. She came into the sun a little way and Alec saw that she was laughing. "And you are sitting on the ground in your clean trousers! Isidro—you infidel!"

Alec stood up slowly and stretched; Isidro got up more rapidly, slapping at his thighs and back sides with his hands.

"It is clean dirt. Observe—it is no dirt at all; it is only the mother earth. I sit on her all my life."

"But I am not washing for you all my life," Lupita scolded. "Mother earth or no, you are not to sit upon her when it is Lupita who is doing the washing."

Alec listened and was amused; and at the same time, without being able to understand the reason, he was lonely.

Now, then, this was the life, all right. There was never a time that Alec could remember when he had had to devote so little conscious effort to relaxing and taking it easy. There never was a time, in the last ten years, anyway, that he'd been able to lie down in the sun and doze, or take a slow walk along the creek, or pleasure himself in any other manner without having his mind creep out ahead of itself, sending feelers of suspicion and doubt and anxiety as to what the next moment or hour might bring. Up here, though, that wasn't hard to do at all. Up here, with all them mountains going straight on up into God's lap, a man got the idea that all his troubles and sins were way behind him and there wasn't anything to think about at all except living on from one day to the next, with each one kind of flowing into the one that followed after. A body got to feeling that he was a pretty humble and unimportant kind of creature and that most of his miserable affairs didn't amount to nothing at all.

And he only had to look through the window at the mountains to know that it was so.

Lord, them mountains were something to look upon! A man never wearied of sittin' out there on the ground just watchin' them things. They had more moods than a strong-minded woman and they never seemed to have the same one twice. A man could sit there with his eyes on them all day long, and far into the evening, too, and he'd be treated to something new every minute of the clock.

It was always changing. One day there might be one of them fast-workin' mountain squalls, with the clouds scudding grey and thick over the peaks, catchin' on them now and then and lettin' the water out with the rain comin' in black sheets down the slopes and across the canyons, and the lightnin' sparklin' yellow fire up and down the cliffs and the thunder hammering away at everything, and the creek swollen up like a man's black eye.

And the next day all that might be gone and it would be hard to imagine from the looks of things up there that there'd ever been a storm at all, because them old peaks were stickin' up there just like they'd been doin' for a million years and there didn't appear to be no change in them, except for the shadows that the sun and clouds were makin'.

They were mostly fleecy clouds when the sun was shining. Sometimes, if a man was to hold his head just right, and maybe squint a little, the cloud he was lookin' at wouldn't be a cloud at all, but one of them new spring lambs, turning its head this way and that like it was lookin' for its mother. Another time the cloud would be a ship, a spankin'-big fightin' ship with a hundred guns on her and sailin' out to sea carrying canvas enough to cover half the Territory. Or maybe there'd be a couple of clouds together, like a pair of heads, with eyes and mouths, and maybe even ears and they'd be floatin' over the hills laughin' with one another and tellin' jokes.

There were other times, though, when the quiet grey clouds were up there shredded on the peaks when the rocky flanks seemed reflective and self-contained like their thinking was far off somewhere dwellin' on things that'd happened a very great while ago. A kind of mood'd come on 'em, then, that wasn't easy for a mortal man to figure out.

Sometimes when the mood was on the mountains, and sometimes when it wasn't, Alec's mind would turn away from their pleasant living up there and he'd become conscious of the moving around of those old unsettling things that still lurked back in amongst his private thoughts.

Mostly he could go for hours, or days even, hunting in the hills, fishing the creek, or maybe the lakes and fast-running streams further up, or helping out with the growing beef stock, or simply basking in the sun before the casa, without being deviled by all those things that had happened down there in the shadow of the Guadeloupes.

But there were other times when remembrance would hammer in his head relentlessly, with a beat as strong and steady as that of an Indian war drum. Maybe he'd be out hunting somewhere in the aspens, admiring the way they seemed to shake and shimmer in the early fall sun, and an animal would make a sly movement in the brush, and right away—without any clear reason for it—his mind would see the Apache sliding around the camp in those slick, flowing movements he used to have. Or maybe he'd be leaning around the evening fire with Isidro crooning melodies on an old guitar he'd bought, and all of a sudden the burning piñon logs would take the shape of the burning cabin upon themselves and he would once again see the yellow-haired woman with her hands pressed to her temples in her screams.

On the other hand it didn't need to be anything like that at all. There didn't always have to be an association of some kind—a graphic tie. These old things would creep up on him, with no warning whatsoever; they'd creep up on him, sometimes, when he was sleeping, and he'd sit bolt upright in bed with the sweat bathing his head and his eyes staring hard at the wooden santo on the white wall, yet not seeing that carved image, but the dark, curved arm and the chevrons of the trooper, lying on his belly at the Black. . . .

He saw the trooper quite a lot at night.

It all ended on a fine October day. For a time, now, an uneasiness had been building up in him—perhaps it had been there all along, he had no way of knowing; but this restiveness had got to be more and more a part of his mental and nervous make-up, and when the end came it was almost with a feeling of relief. The first months had been good and fine and he had got to feeling that he was doing the things that a man was made for, but during the early weeks of fall, after they'd learned from tales coming up the trail that Stone and Clint were still alive and on the prowl, he'd come to realize that his mountain living was only a temporary thing. He'd got to thinking that it was a luxury that he could not afford just yet, and that Clint and Stone were a sort of reckoning that must be met. So, that fine October day was as good a one as any.

"Ho, the chili we will have this winter," Isidro was saying. "It will have peppers enough to burn the top of your head off. We will turn your hair red and keep it that way as long as you live."

Alec had just then seen Nino and he did not reply. Nino and the burro were a hundred yards and more away from them and the sun made a bright glare upon the white trousers and shirt which the boy was wearing. The burro was moving slowly and obstinately and presently Nino got down and pulled at the halter about the animal's head. The orphan boy appeared to be greatly impatient to get to them.

"He will get nowhere doing that," Isidro observed. "That burro is in league with the devil himself."

"I got a pair of rowels that'd make him move," Alec said. Nino had now braced his bare heels into the ground and the rope was taut as he bent backwards.

"Not that one," Isidro said. "His soul is as black as Lupita's hair. When Hernan sold him to Pike he confided the ancestry of that creature to me," Isidro clucked his tongue without elaborating.

"I still say my rowels'd make him kite."

"No, you could rake his flanks to the bone . . . there, see? Regard Nino. He had sense at that."

Whether it was sense or urgency, Alec could not immediately tell because Nino was still too far away for his expression to be seen, but he had now thrown the halter rope upon the ground in disgust and commenced to run up the trail, his brown feet making little explosions in the dust.

"It must be very urgent," Isidro said. "I do not think Nino run very much."

Alec was about to say, yes, it must be urgent, indeed, but then he didn't because Nino had gotten close enough to them for Alec to get a clear look at his face. Nino was a gangling boy with a carefree frame of mind and whenever he and Pike would come to visit he would entertain them with his strange dances and the quaint songs he had learned. Nino had a long, pleasant face which never seemed to lose the reflection of his happy nature, but coming up the trail, now, his long feet slapping in the dirt, his features were the embodiment of tragedy. He was breathless when he reached them, and everything came out of him at once, in a torrent, as Isidro caught him and kept him from stumbling to his knees.

"They have come!" Nino gasped in a moment. "They, the bad ones have come! Señor Pike is dead! They have killed him, he is dead!"

It was then that Alec became wholly conscious of the beauty of the day. Never before had the sky seemed so deeply blue or the few clouds so pristine in their whiteness. The mountain had a clear-cut majesty which was hard for a man's mind to grasp, and the beauty of the creek and the aspens and the cottonwood and the peppers above the doorway was compelling beyond imagination. He was not entirely certain why he became so aware of those things at just that time, unless perhaps it was an intimation that he was looking at them all for the last time. . . .

• CHAPTER 9 •
Meeting in the Sun

IT MADE NO DIFFERENCE THAT LUPITA WEPT HERSELF LIMP as a rag—Isidro went with Alec anyway. They argued about it all the way down to the main trail and they were nearly to Pike's place above Las Vegas before Alec was reconciled to it.

"It ain't none of your business down there at Pike's," Alec had said.

"It is so my business," Isidro had said. "Everywhere is my business."

"It ain't either," Alec had retorted. "It ain't your affair nohow. You got a wife and a house and young ones comin', for all I know, and you got the cattle to take care of."

"That is nothing when there is this," Isidro had said.

"Maybe the cattle know about it? Did you explain it to them?"

"I renounce them," Isidro had said. "Until we return I renounce them."

"You got no business to think of anything else," Alec had said. "You ain't a free man no more."

"No? Well, it is still my business; if it is yours so it is mine. So long as they live it is mine as it is yours. They are not dead, as we thought, so the other things do not matter."

Isidro's saying that put Alec's mind on the day when they had divined that Clint and Stone were alive. How those two had ever got away from the posse at the cabin fire there was no way of knowing unless they were to be asked about it. Alec was not even sure how he and Isidro got away. Everything after the killing of the Apache was a kind of blue in his memory. It was all confused with the horses running and Roy sliding to the ground, the brilliant searing of flame leaping away in the night, the gunfire beyond the cabin and the sheets of pain from the wound made by the Apache's knife.

After that there had been the steady march north—Isidro always leading and himself drooping across the saddle pommel, sometimes clutching at the mane of the horse and always cursing Isidro for subjecting him to this torment. But they never stopped. North, always north: Hondo, Lincoln, Corona, Encino, Villaneuva, Mora—into the belly of the Sangre de Cristos. Isidro had been very grim in his determination.

Like as not, Stone and Clint had made it clear in much the same way. Like as not, the posse had thought first to fight its way through to the cabin to see if anyone was left alive, expecting to attend to the marauders later. Perhaps, too, upon discovering the bodies of Roy and the Apache, and recalling what had befallen another posse having the temerity to track the desperados into the hills at night, they had been momentarily content with their bag of two dead.

It really made little difference how those two had happened to elude the vigilantes—it was the fact that they had which held importance. It was the fact they had and that after staying on the dodge for the whole of the summer the particular type of mark they ordinarily left on a job began to appear here and there, and finally to take a slow course toward the north.

Alec had tried to analyze his feelings when he'd first figured out Stone and Clint's being alive. He surely wasn't happy about it, and on the other hand he hadn't been unduly concerned about it.

When they had passed beyond Mora and were nearing Sapello Isidro pushed the index finger of his right hand into the trigger guard of his gun, and eased it up slightly in the holster. They had brought the horses down to a walk for the last of the trip and Isidro's adjusting of the gun was calculated and deliberate. It made Alec stare at him hard, and to become once more aware that, of all of them, only Isidro— and perhaps Pike to a lesser degree—had made the transition; that only Isidro's life had developed the kind of continuity which would let him live his years as a happy man. Alec had known for quite awhile that he was beyond a thing like that himself.

Sapello had become a crude cluster of buildings clearly in their vision when Alec began to argue with Isidro again. He had seen a small, timbered cantina, somewhat detached from those of the town, and nearer along the road, in front of which two horses were lazing in the sun. One of those was an old paint horse which he remembered very well. Stone always took a heap of pride in that animal's endurance.

"Once more, Isidro, this ain't your affair," Alec said.

"You are wrong," Isidro said without looking at him. "It is mine as well as yours."

"Isidro, there ain't much time."

"I know. I observe the paint horse. I think we walk now, no?"

Alec got down on the road and watched Isidro shoo the horses off to the side. When he came back he was smiling softly, and beyond them the door of the cantina was opening. Clint and Stone came out leisurely, then paused as they looked up the road. They were still a hundred feet away, but the wariness in them was plain to see.

"I think we are here," Isidro said.

"Yeah," Alec said. "We're here, all right."

They all understood what the meeting was about and there was no talk, no preliminaries. Stone and Clint took in the meaning without any visible show of surprise or astonishment, and moved slowly, a few paces apart, toward the center of the dusty road. When they stopped there was maybe ten feet between them, Clint nearer to the building, with the shade from the sagging overhead gallery cutting a sharp line near his feet, and Stone directly in the sun, with his hat brim pulled down tight, making a dark patch across the upper part of his face. Neither one had changed much, that Alec could see, though he could not think why he had supposed they might have.

Stone still had that lowering, mean look, which, sullen though it was, didn't always give any indication of what he might be going to do. Stone still wore those dirty old clothes—dark pants stuffed into his scuffed boots, faded, shapeless shirt, so steeped in sweat and weather that it was hard to tell if it had ever had any true color at all, battered soiled hat, grooved in the brim where he had jerked at it, and nearly black with hair grease around the lower part of the crown. Stone's meaty face always seemed to need a shave, and that hadn't changed either.

Clint, now, there was a slight alteration in him—a kind of seasoned quality, a kind of set to his face and head that didn't quite tally up with the remembrance of him in Alec's mind. The last time he'd seen

Clint there'd been that hair spiking through the bandage and his face had been peaked from the fever caused by the crease along his skull. There was still a sharpness there, though, caused by his bones having too much edge, and maybe helped along some by his eagerness to kill.

Clint, Alec thought, would make the break; Clint would be the first one to try for his gun. Clint didn't have the temperament to play a waiting game.

Behind Stone, a small bird flickered through the air, then swung off the road and Alec caught the movement of it in the tail of his eye as it went by him and away. Birds had always held a fascination for him. The freedom that a bird had was all that any man could ever hope for, and yet it was a hopeless kind of thing to hanker after because a man's pursuit of it was bound to be a stumbling, blundering chase; most always, he lost in the end. A man had to be awfully strong inside to keep his sights up where he'd put them in the first place.

Alec was still thinking about the bird when Clint's shoulder and arm jerked and his gun came out. Alec was still thinking about the bird and remembering another one, skimming toward the surface of the Black, and seeing the trooper silent on the ground, when Clint's gun came out and the whole road seemed to jump dust in the sound that followed.

He was watching Clint particularly, but when the sound shattered everything Clint was a part of the whole and the sound of Clint's gun was only a small portion of the sound of all the guns which filled the road and high, hot sunlight with the roaring of creation and the end of all things on earth. Alec had not been aware of the physical movement of drawing and thumbing the hammer, but he must have done it because he felt his finger on the trigger and the strength of the spring beneath his thumb and the stag-horn butt bucking against the palm of his hand.

And he heard Isidro's gun shouting beside him and saw Clint lift slightly as though he was going to begin a dance and then turn and walk stiffly and blindly into Stone, who was already falling, but still firing with both hands holding his gun and his knees bent and wide to hold him up. And he saw them tumble into an awkward heap and wondered weirdly why he could not move, but then saw his own gun in the dust and felt Isidro grab him as the cold flooded up his legs and the warmth of the sun was no longer on his neck.

The lights were going out and he was going under. Isidro was talking to him but Isidro's voice was very far away and soon he could not hear it any longer and there was only great quiet and darkness closing out the light; the darkness, deep and vacant and nothing at all—nothing, until in a far off place the chevronned sleeve of the trooper lay reaching across the ground, and his own hand stretching toward it, groping, clawing, and touching it at last.

Isidro was sitting in front of the evening fire with the boy Nino when he saw the shadows of the horsemen coming up the trail. They were already quite close and as he placed the guitar on the ground and came around the fire to greet them he saw that there were eight of them and that they were troopers. When they reined up they did not dismount, but looked warily about them in the gathering darkness, except for the leader, a corporal, who spoke to Isidro.

"We're lookin' for a fight; you know anything about a fight?"

"A fight, Señor-Capitán? We have no fight here."

The corporal cleared his throat. "Not here. I'm talkin' about the one down near Sapello two days ago. A gunfight. I'm tryin' to find out who knows about it."

Isidro shook his head slowly and looked at Nino. "Have you heard of this fight, Nino?"

The boy gathered his sarape about his shoulders and stared at the troopers. "No, Isidro. But no, I hear of no such fight."

The corporal looked around before he spoke again. "Can't say I wonder much," he said then. "Sure seems quiet up here." Then in a burst of confidence he grinned boyishly at Isidro. "Nice place you got. Wouldn't be surprised if I'd try and find me a spot like it when my time's up."

"It is very nice here," Isidro said.

"Yeah, it sure is. A beautiful evenin', too."

"Sí, yes," Isidro said.

When the corporal got his troop headed off down the trail again Isidro sat down once more and picked up the guitar, strumming at it idly while he watched the horses merge with the gloom below. Gradually, the words of a song he had one time heard came into his head and found their way to his tongue—the music filling his fingers upon the strings.

Get six jolly cowboys to carry my coffin;
Get six pretty maidens to bear up my pall;
Put bunches of roses all over my coffin,
Put roses to deaden the clods as they fall.

Then swing your rope slowly and rattle your spurs
    lowly,
And give a wild whoop as you bear me along;
And in the grave throw me, and roll the sod over
    me,
For I'm a young cowboy, and I know I've done
    wrong . . .

Isidro was filled with a poignant sadness as he stopped the singing and watched Lupita come out of the casa and look at him with her secretive smile.

Yes, surely she was more round these days; would there be twins?

"Did the soldiers want Alec?"

"Quién sabe? Perhaps."

"They would do better to ask of the Diós for him."

"Sí, yes, they would."

"Isidro, are you cold out here?"

"No, muchacha; we have the fire. But soon we come inside."

Lupita returned to the casa and Isidro picked up the guitar, then thought better of it and laid it down. Instead, he selected a piñone from a little pile between himself and Nino, and cracked it loudly between his teeth. All around the night was falling very quickly now, and only on the highest peaks was the sun striking in golden splendor upon the snow. The corporal had been right, Isidro thought. The evening was very beautiful, indeed. . . .

THE HARD ONE

• CHAPTER 1 •
Powdersmoke in his Eyes

It was nearly noon of a clean summer day when the Santa Fe chuffed into Vegas and Clay Forest stepped down from the coach and saw Efigio Varga waiting for him with the roan horse strung on a lead behind his own. For a moment he had the notion that nothing had ever changed at all and that those two years passed over in time had been qualities of his imagination; the roan horse looked pretty much as he always had—the clean, red lines and high-sheened coat—and Efigio had not altered either. Except for the attitude of caution—occasioned by the nature of the moment—Efigio was no different than he had been at any time before.

Efigio blew his nose violently and shook Clay's hand with heartiness. "Clay! Señor Clay, how are you? Señor Clay, you look like a million pesos. On the railroad you come, and we are waiting for you here!"

"It's all right, Efigio, it's all right."

"Como no, it is bueno for certain. We are here, yes, and now we are all together and going home. Regard the Morgan—see how happy he is to see you."

"It's all right," Clay said again. "Don't get so damned excited. Everything's all right."

Clay let Efigio's hand slip out of his own and stood near the Morgan. For a long moment the red horse looked at him, then dipped its head and nuzzled his hands. The warm velvet breathed against his palms and the hurt inside him for a time gave way before the remembrance of old associations. How long ago had Pa given him the Morgan? Three years? Three was close enough, but it was nearer to a lifetime now; yet his recollection of the occasion was as clear and fresh and unsullied by the intervening incidents as though it had happened only yesterday. There never was a horse like that Morgan Pa had got him; unless it was the one that Pa himself had ridden at his death.

Clay rubbed the long bones in the arched nose, slapped the solid neck and went around and tugged at the cinch. He put his foot into the stirrup and swung on up; he grinned as he felt the leather slap solid at his backsides.

"I reckon that's pretty good, ain't it?" Clay said. "I been needin' somethin' like this for quite awhile."

Efigio was laughing loudly as he threw his leg across the cantle of his saddle. "Sí, you look fine, Clay. You look like a great rico on that horse. Only before I come up here from the ranch I say to Lupe, I say, 'that Clay, that young señor, will be the greatest caballero in the whole of New Mexico upon that horse. Ho! How he will look!'"

Clay walked the Morgan for a few paces down the dusty street before he said anything. He had it straight in his own mind and he had to get it that way in Efigio's. There was no sense in dilly-dallying around. He couldn't have Efigio carrying on like a two-year-old, behaving like he never had before.

"You can take it easy now, Efigio," he said. "It's all right, you can calm down. You don't have to tear your head off makin' me welcome. I'm a jailbird. You know it and I know it, so let's get used to it and be natural. It's two years out of my life and I'm willin' to forget it and take up where I left off. Savvy?"

Efigio relieved himself of a big breath of air. "Sí, I savvy. Sí, Clay, I understand how you feel. I simply want you to feel good inside. I want you to know I am glad to see you again."

Clay dropped the Morgan back. "I know you're glad to see me, and I appreciate it; I guess there ain't nothin' in the world like good friends. And, don't you go worryin' 'bout me feelin' good; I reckon I feel pretty good, all right."

Clay nearly always felt clumsy when trying to express emotion and he experienced a vague sense of relief when Efigio seemed to recognize it and accept it. Efigio smiled again and Clay knew he had put it right.

"Now, then," he said, "how's it back home? You don't need to spare me none. Give me the worst; I'm expectin' it."

Efigio tugged at his soiled hat and wiped his hand across his ragged mustachios. "Well, well, I do not think it is so very good back there. I have trouble in the round-up. There are some cattle missing, and there are not as many of the calves as I think we should have. And I cannot get the men to help. I have one or two, and sometimes, even three, but they do not stay; and anyway, they are not ones to have for long."

"Rustlin'?" Clay said.

"Maybe," Efigio said. "Perhaps. But mostly it is because there is no one to help. The cattle, they get notions and they wander off and there is no one to bring them back. I do my best, Clay, but . . . well . . . you know how it can be . . ."

Clay spoke without looking at Efigio. His eyes were rambling from side to side along the street, passing from this weathered building to that. Everything looked drowsy and without energy in the sun and stillness of the day. Down the street some, a young boy, maybe ten or twelve, was watching them solemnly as they came along, a solitary sign of life in the heat and quiet.

"I thought we was agreed we was goin' to speak right out with none of this fancy side-steppin'," Clay said. "What you mean is, you can't get nobody good to work on the place 'cause everyone knows it's Forest property and their minds is set against us."

"Well, I do not like to say that right out, Clay, but it is that, I think." Efigio pulled up abreast of Clay and peered into his face, as though to compensate with his manner for the reality of the spoken words.

"Well, you got to be direct about it," Clay said. "We ain't never goin' to get nowhere 'less you recognize what's what. In the eyes of them on the Pecos I'm a criminal and there ain't no good comin' in failin' to see it that way."

"I do not think you are bad," Efigio said with feeling. "The trial, it was wrong, and you are not bad."

"Well, I know I ain't neither," Clay said. "But I done a lot of thinkin' on it in the prison there, and I figure the best thing is to let things be and the devil with what people think. No amount of talk's goin' to change anything. There's that other business anyway; that Robey business. And they ain't goin' to forget about that soon."

Clay turned slightly in his saddle when he said this and he was startled by the sad cast of Efigio's face. It made him feel a slow wonder at the great capacity for loyalty in the Mexican; it made him think that there were not many who would put up with what

Efigio had in the years since Hardin Forest's death. The Pecos people didn't take kindly to a man who sided a convicted criminal.

Clay got a note of kindness into his tone to cover up the brittle feeling in him. "I expect that ain't all that's happened while I was gone," he said. "No doubt Robey and some of his has been around."

"Sí, they come," Efigio admitted. "They come three, maybe four times. They come and ask about you and then they go away again."

"They take anything? They run off any stock?"

"No, I do not think they do that," Efigio said. "But the people on the river, the people, when they learn that Robey and his have been to the ranch, are angry; and they say bad things about you again."

Clay glared at the white dust boiling around the Morgan's feet. "Let 'em," he said. "Let 'em say what they blame well please; yeah, and let 'em think it, too."

That time there was a long silence between them and they were nearly to the place where the young boy was lounging against the gallery post of one of the grey, tired buildings when Efigio looked at Clay apologetically.

"Clay," he said, "Clay, maybe it is best to sell your place. I will stay with you and work for you as I did for your father, and you know that, Clay, but it will not be a happy place for you with the feeling like it is. There are those, I think, who would like your land, and would pay for it if you would sell it. The Señor Liston one time said he would give a good price."

Clay laughed without humor. "Dodge Liston, huh? Good old self-righteous Dodge. Pious-speakin' goat."

Efigio shrugged and rubbed the top of his saddle pommel with his hand. "Sí, yes, he is a great one with words and large thoughts, but he said he would pay for the land, and that is something."

"With all the money and land he's got he still

wants more," Clay said. "Some ain't never satisfied, I guess."

Clay was looking ahead again. He was watching the young boy against the gallery post and he saw that the kid was regarding them in a peculiar and wary way. He was nothing more than a sandy-haired youngster, gangling and kind of gawky the way that kids get at that age, but there was in his manner the special kind of caution that Clay had known people to have when they knew they were looking at him. Clay's horse was nearly abreast of the boy when he suddenly turned and shouted into the doorway in back of him.

"Hey! It's Clay Forest! The Moore gang is here! Clay Forest's ridin' in and the Robey Moore gang is here! Gawdalmighty, he's comin' down the street!"

Clay felt his insides jerk. The shock of it went all the way through him and down to his boots. A quick, cold panic yelled in his stomach; he wanted to run, to break out and ride like crazy beyond the sound of that voice; out of that town and away and on and on until the roan horse fell exhausted. Beside him, Efigio Varga swore, ranged up close and brought his gun out, then let it drop as Clay brought his hand across his wrist. The panic had gone as quickly as it had come and Clay sat ramrod straight as the Vegas people bobbed their heads through doors and windows.

"Look at him!" a voice called from an upstairs window. "Forest! By God, it is Forest!"

"See him? Right there! On the roan horse!"

A buxom woman scuttled across the road, her feet impelled by terror and down a side street the voice of the boy was chanting in a high, shrill wail. "The Moore gang is here! The killers have come!"

On a gallery roof, the querulous voice of an old man picked it up. "Clay Forest is ridin' in! Forest, the murderin' scum, is ridin' in!"

"Sapristi!" Efigio said: "These goats! I tell them. Efigio Varga will tell them."

"No, you won't," Clay said. "I'll tell 'em. It's me they're talkin' about."

He jerked around again; he saw the heads and moving, vacant faces—the expressions of apprehension and secret enjoyment and morbid curiosity. He saw them all at once and they were all the same, a composite of animal instinct and herd psychology. It made him take a kind of fierce and twisted pleasure in the sensation he was creating. It made him almost wish that everything they said was true. It made him laugh and shout and yell abuse at them.

"You damned right it's Clay Forest! I'm ridin' through your stinkin' town and there ain't a man among you that can stop me! I'll take on you yellow-bellies ten at a time and the rest of you gutless buzzards can have the leavings!"

Clay swung around in the saddle, ripped his jacket off and waved it overhead. The hot, crazy madness was in his head and he couldn't stop it now. Everything was there in a tortured jumble of long-gone, bitter things restored to life with hate and passion— the black days of the Lincoln fight, the killing of Hardin, the rapacity of Robey Moore and the long days in prison for a crime he hadn't done.

"Look here!" he yelled. "See? I ain't even packin' a gun! You know why? I don't need one, that's why! I don't need one 'cause I can kill with my eyes!"

• CHAPTER 2 •
The Wild Whirlwind

THEY TOOK THEIR TIME GOING FROM LAS VEGAS DOWN TO the plainsland on the lower Pecos. They took their time and Clay was in no particular hurry because he had long since gotten over being in a hurry for anything. It never seemed to pay to more than take things as they came.

They rode through fine country in those days. They rode through high timber and deep meadows, across broad flanks of hills, and wide valleys, green with water and lush with promise. They rode through towns and villages—Los Montoyas, Anton Chico, Dilia, Santa Rosa—towns which might have been there for a hundred years and more for all anyone knew, and whose origins were buried in the antiquity of Spanish conquest. They followed the river into the plains and on to the south, through spreading flats of memory and old associations. They passed beneath the barracks of old Fort Sumner, and beyond the town where Billy Antrim, alias Bonney, alias the

Kid, lay sleeping in the dust. Antrim, yes, and Charlie Bowdre, too. And Tom O'Folliard; Pat Garret's work.

Beyond Fort Sumner, they bent due south and left the river for awhile. They had been on the move for most of five days and they were getting into country which had the smell of home about it. Far to the west and southwest, the Jicarillas and Capitans and Sacramentos crashed their peaks against the sky and filled Clay with the renewed wonder of their creation; and with the old, unhappy contemplation of the things which had happened in their shadows. Most of all the grief and trouble in his life had had its generation in those mountains. They were where the biggest share of the Lincoln war had been fought; and in their pine-shot bellies was where his Pa had died.

In the beginning, he remembered, there was the Pecos war and then the Harrold war and finally, the biggest of all, the Lincoln war. The first had commenced in the early seventies when John Chisum brought his Jingle Bob brand up the lower Pecos cattle trails from the heart of Texas, but soon they got mixed up and twisted in men's minds and the whole, bloody ten years of chaos and upheaval got lumped together under the name of the last of these.

It had loud repercussions in distant places. It brought wails of anguish and indignation from nester-folk, and it brought a new governor for the Territory. It brought a kind of half-hearted intervention from the federal troopers at Fort Stanton and other posts, and it acquired a semblance of an international complication when John Tunstall, the English cattleman, got in the way of Billy Morton's posse. Those Britishers did not seem to understand that a man carried the statutes on his hip in the country beyond the wide Missouri; and that it was the court of last resort, from which there was no appeal known to Anglo-Saxon law.

A good many folks thereabouts thought Hardin Forest was a fool to get himself mixed up in that business in the first place. Clay sometimes wondered if there might not be an element of truth in their hasty estimation, but then he would feel shamed at having such a thought, because his Pa was a strong man who had definite ideas as to what was right and what was wrong.

He kept good cattle and horses and treated them with consideration. He would spend a winter's night, if need be, riding through the chaparral in search of a strayed-off yearling. And on the nights when he was not doing things like that he would read to them all from the family Bible by the light of an oil lamp in the home ranch on the lower Pecos. He was Kentucky-bred and he had powerful convictions in his heart. There was nobody going to push him around if he could help it. No hired gunhand from Mexico-way, or anywhere else, was going to ease him off his land.

When the Lincoln war exploded out of the Pecos and Harrold preliminaries, he sided up with those avenging John Tunstall's wanton slaughter. For a time he rode with Dick Brewer's posse, leg and leg with the worst gun-toughs in that or any other territory. He shared chow in many a dark camp with Tom Hill, John Middleton, Dave Rudabaugh, Doc Skurlock, Bowdre, O'Folliard, Ike Stockton and the blue-eyed, boy-smiling Billy the Kid, but he always kept his Bible with him.

A year later Robey Moore came on the dodge from the south of Texas and took a hand in the way of life that he liked best. He was as competent with a gun as a man can be and Hardin Forest was shrewd enough to recognize it. Without changing allegiance, he switched to Robey's newly-organized contingent. That same year he bought the Morgans and gave Clay to understand that he could ride with the posse if he so chose.

This occurred on the day of Clay Forest's eighteenth birthday, and he was too young to understand the tangled web he wove. A week later, Hardin Forest was clawing his last breath from the pine-braced air of the Ruidoso country, and Clay was signed on with Robey Moore for better or for worse. He had sown the wind, and so must reap the wild whirlwind.

Clay always remembered the day that Hardin died. For beauty, the untempered air of the Ruidoso timber had no peer in his mind or memory, and its splendor was at its most compelling on the morning of that fatal day. They had kept a cold camp on property owned jointly by Charlie Bowdre and Doc Skurlock and they were awake and on the lookout as dawn washed red and gold among the trees about them. They were expecting trouble.

Hardin Forest had put the two Morgans into hobbles for the night and Clay went out to bring them in. There had been none awake but himself and Diamond-Back, the night guard, when he went out, but coming back he found them all stretching out of sleep and getting ready for what they knew was coming.

"I figure these two will prove their worth this day," Hardin said as Clay brought the roans and got ready to saddle up. Hardin stood there in his long underwear and trousers and boots and his face had a clean-cut steady look about it even through the growth of whiskers. "You scared, son?"

Clay was deliberate with putting the bit into the Morgan's mouth. "I guess I'm scared, all right, but I ain't scared in a way that'd make me run off."

"That's all right, then," Hardin said. "If you'd told

me you wasn't, I'd of known you was lyin'. Every man's scared the first time."

"You think there's goin' to be somethin' big, Pa?" Clay said. Clay kept busy with the saddle and harness and tried to be casual.

"Can't say for sure just yet, but Robey's got the feel of it. Stands to reason, though, that Murphy bunch ain't goin' to let us sashay out of here without somethin'. Not after what was done to Baker and Billy Morton."

Clay turned around and looked at his Pa. Hardin's whiskers had a high shine in the sun coming through the trees. "We didn't have nothin' to do with killin' them," Clay said. "That was Skurlock and Bowdre and McNab and that Bonney feller they call the Kid."

"It don't make no difference, Clay," Hardin said. "It's all the same. We're all in it together."

Pretty soon they had the horses and gear ready and Robey came back from scouting around and they all talked it over. He'd had Ed Picket out there with him and they'd spotted the Murphy bunch working up the creek from the east. They'd likely come out in a wide arc from Lincoln, Robey said, and was figuring on coming upon them in surprise.

The thing about Robey Moore was in his eyes. He wasn't much to look at otherwise. He was kind of sloppy in his dress and manner, never cleaned up very much, or shaved or anything like that, and didn't look so very different than anybody else. But when you looked him in the face you got a kind of chill inside. Some folks said a man's eyes was the windows to his soul, but if that was true then Robey didn't have a soul, nohow. His eyes was as empty and vacant as a dried out well.

After Robey told them what was up and said they'd split and take the Murphy bunch from either side they broke it up and climbed aboard. Bod Fergus and Ed Picket and Diamond-Back and Steve Howard were going to go off into the deep timber and wait and the others were going to go around and stir things up when the Murphy crowd came up.

"I figure you Forests better stay with me," Robey Moore said when they were ready. Robey swung his eyes around the small clearing they had camped in, then took a long look at Clay. Clay hitched at his belt.

"How you feel, kid?" Robey said.

Clay sat straight in the saddle and ran his hand along the Morgan's neck. "Why, I guess I feel pretty good. How do you feel?"

Robey allowed himself a dry laugh, and looked around some more. Robey was always looking around, like he suspected every motion in the brush.

"You sound spunky, all right," he said then. "Hope you show like you talk."

"I won't turn tail if that's what you mean."

"You just do what you're told and everything'll be all right."

"I figure I can do that," Clay said. He wished the devil they'd get through gabbing and be on with it. Wasn't right for Robey to be putting all that talk at him at a time like this. It made him feel like a stewing hen that was being poked to see if it was done or not.

"All right, then," Robey said, "we better git."

They rode on out. At the edge of the clearing the waiting party crossed the Ruidoso and went into the timber on the other side. Clay followed his Pa and Robey straight up the bank and then they made a big turn and back-tracked down below the place where they had camped. They were going directly into the big, gold sun and Clay had never seen a thing like that before. The whole forest was full of color and the carpet was soft and spongy underfoot. In the high trees the birds were calling and scampering here and there and not far off the creek was splashing and spilling over the rocks in drops and streaks of copper. It made a body want to go right over there and get the feel of it around his feet and ankles.

In a little bit Robey went on ahead to look around and Clay picked the Morgan's gait up so he could ride beside his Pa. They went in quiet for quite a spell and then Hardin commenced to talk.

"You stick with Robey and you'll be all right," Hardin said presently. "Should anything happen, you stick with him 'till this is done. Then there'll be the ranch for you."

Clay felt something get into his back and make him sit straighter. It wasn't the kind of tone that Hardin used, except when he was maybe reading from the Bible, and it made him take a slow, sidewise look at him.

"Why, I reckon I am stickin' with him, ain't I?" he said. "We both are."

"Sure, I know we are, but just the same, you do like I say. You stick with him. He'll get you through this if anyone can. He may be just another gunslinger to a lot of folks, and maybe his end'll be like all the others, but I figure he'll last through this business."

Clay turned it over in his head and tried to sort it out. It seemed almost that Hardin was slipping away from him, going off to a place that he couldn't trail him to, but there was no time to explore all the implications because Robey came busting back to them through the trees and reined up in a flurry in front of them.

"Damn it," Robey said, "they're onto it. We got to work this different. They split up just like we did. We got to get back to the others. Come on, let's go!" Robey's bay gelding danced and shied and Robey called across his shoulder as he sank the spurs in deep. "Come on, dammit, let's go! Let's go!"

The shooting broke out before they'd gone a hundred yards and Clay could hear it cracking and echoing among the trees ahead of them. He was pressed warm against the soft coat of the Morgan's neck and the muscles underneath him spread and expanded against his chest, and against his face when he would put it there. In between the shooting bursts he could hear the soft pounding of the roan's hooves beneath him, and sometimes those of Robey's horse beyond him, and those of Hardin's to his rear.

When the split part of the Murphy bunch stumbled onto them, Clay was not aware of it until he heard the sudden sound of the close-in gunfire and the blending scream of the Morgan Hardin rode. Then it hit him all at once and he was conscious of the shadows racing through the trees to the side and to the rear, of the streaks of light bursting bright and vivid from the green and brown and of Hardin spilling to the ground beneath his horse.

Clay swung his own around without knowing he had done it and sent the roan crashing back toward Hardin. Vaguely, above the sound of the shooting he heard Robey yelling profanely at him, but he kept on going back. He was close to Hardin now. He could see how he was pinned and how he was wrenching his gun. The Morgan heaved and tossed in agony and each motion of the heavy horse brought a lighter shade of grey to Hardin's features.

The other rider exploded through the brush as Clay was swinging down. Clay saw the double-barreled shotgun spring from the saddle scabbard and he felt the sickest, coldest fear he ever had before or after that engulf him as the yawning muzzles smashed flame and lead into Hardin's tossing body. He saw the brown, young face and the eyes as thin as leaves of grass behind the polished stock and then he saw those same eyes glaze and splash red and messy as the slugs from his Colt tore the rider from his saddle and hammered him into the ground and soft pine-needle covering. Clay fanned the hammer of the Colt in a roar and sheet of flame and when it was empty and clicking dry he raised the gun and pistol-whipped the body at his feet. He was still standing there, numb and halfway senseless, when Robey swung up and threw himself to the ground.

"I thought I told you to come with me!" Robey Moore was shouting. "I thought you was going to do like I say! What you doin' here?"

The things that Robey was saying did not register with Clay and he could only gape at him like someone who was not familiar with the language he was hearing. He felt like he was made of wood or stone and when his arm moved in an indefinite arc toward Hardin's body it did not seem that it belonged to him at all. Even when Robey hit him he did not feel it, or when he glanced against the giant pine or rolled on the ground and pushed drunkenly to his hands and knees.

And over and over the fine, clean air of the Ruidoso timber carried the rage of Robey's voice.

"I'll learn yuh, Forest! I'll learn yuh to do what I say! I'll learn yuh who gives orders in this outfit! By God, you ain't never goin' to fergit again!"

• CHAPTER 3 •
Old Ghosts

ON THE EIGHTH DAY FROM VEGAS EFIGIO AND CLAY pulled over the slow rise above the Forest land and buildings and eased their horses toward the spreading cottonwoods, strong and fertile in a long lane toward the dooryard. A slow catch came into Clay's throat when they turned into it and he saw Lupe's attentive and generous-proportioned figure shading her eyes toward them from the gallery at the far end. She gave a low cry as the two horses came out of the lane and walked through the sun of the court, and half-dragged Clay from the saddle when they stopped at last.

"Caramba, Señor Clay! Caramba, you are skin and bones! They have starved you near to death in that place!"

"No, they ain't, Lupe. No, they ain't," Clay said. "It wasn't that bad." He grinned down into Lupe's round face and felt the clean warmth of home coming into him again.

"It is so," Lupe said. Lupe's strong fingers prodded his ribs, pinched his arms and thighs. "Look! There! Your shanks are bare! Bare as a picked shoat. You are naked!"

Clay evaded Lupe's groping hands and commenced to remove the saddle and blanket from the back of the Morgan. "I ain't neither naked," he said. "I even growed some in that place. I stretched out. I just ain't so fat and kid-like any more."

"Ho, it is food you need," Lupe persisted. "Efigio, you fool of all the fools, why did you not feed him? You bring him home like a shadow."

Efigio hung his saddle on the tie rail. "What should I do, muchacha, push the food into his throat with my fist? He eats what he pleases. Who will do more? I think it is as he said. He is simply bigger in some places than before, and not so big in the others."

"Madre de Diós, you men, you will be the death of youselves. A blind man could see he is shrinking into the ground." Lupe regarded Clay with a final, pitying glance before returning to the house. "Food is what he needs! Food, food—enchiladas and tortillas, and chicos, and good, hot chili! Sí, yes, food!"

When she had gone Clay set the saddle and gear on the rail and sent the Morgan off with a slap on the flank. He took an easy turn around the yard, kicking his boots into the ground and getting the feel of the place in his feet and body once again. From the rail, Efigio regarded him with an expression of solemn doubt, as though wondering in his mind what kind of verdict Clay might render on his care of the place during the past two years.

Well, Efigio had done what he could, all right, and Clay could see that no one could have done much better with the kind of transient help he'd had. A man in Efigio's place couldn't very well look after the herd and the buildings, too, and of the whole lot the cattle held the most importance. The buildings

could be gotten after now that he was back. They
weren't too bad; anyway, not so bad that the most
of them couldn't be fixed up proper with time and
effort.

"You done all right, Efigio," he said after a moment, and Efigio appeared relieved. "I guess maybe
we can get back on our feet after a bit; providin' we
can get some help out here."

Efigio curled a wisp of his mustachio around a finger. "Well, you know what I tell you coming from
Vegas; but we can try."

"Yeah, we'll get someone," Clay said. "I'll get after
it right away." He dug his heel into the earth and
twisted it, then grinned at Efigio. "Pronto, Efigio.
Muy pronto."

They went in and had something to eat. If Clay had
had any doubts as to Lupe's concern with his state
of being they would have been dispelled. She piled
food in front of him until he had all he could do to
find a place on the table for his elbows. There was
everything he could think of, and prepared in a manner that he had not been treated to in a longer time
than he now cared to recall.

It put him in mind of the things his father, Hardin,
used to say so long ago. "You got to watch that Lupe,
Clay," he used to say. "Clay, you got to keep your
eye on that mujer 'less she fill you so you can't sit
on your horse right; you're liable to topple right over
sidewise. She's got a fixation in her head about a
man bein' comfortable in his trousers. A body just
don't look right to that woman 'less he's waddlin'
along half drugged from all that food."

And Hardin had been right for certain. There
seemed to be no end of it in sight. Every time Clay
dipped his fork into his plate, or scooped up a load
of chili from the bowl she was right there filling up

the dent he'd made; and all the while crowing at him in a tone of great impatience.

"Eat, skeleton! How can you live if you don't eat? How can you have the strength to lift your hand? Bones! Nothing but bones!"

At last it was done. Clay sank back into the hide-covered chair in a heavy torpor, and looked around. He was filled to a point of pain and discomfiture, but perhaps the orgy had served a purpose at that. It was the first time he was wholly relaxed since he had gone to prison; and through no effort of his own.

The furnishings of that room had not been changed since the premature death of his mother in his early childhood, and were thus related to his earliest recollections of life in that vast country. After she had gone Hardin had not suffered a single change in their arrangement to be made. Clay understood the reason for this to be partly because of Hardin's great devotion to her and his desire to be surrounded by those things which had meant much to her. But he also knew that Hardin had experienced a sense of guilt at those early hardships and uncertainties which had contributed to her early end, and perhaps that had had something to do with it as well.

Except for the wall-prints and the blue-tinted china and the needlepoint-covered sofa, which had been brought on out from Kentucky in the wagon, everything else had been made right there of such native materials as fell to hand. In that early time, much of which was only a misty running together of incidents in Clay's mind, they had whip-sawed pine and cottonwood puncheons for the floors and planks and other pieces for the tables and the bedsteads and doors and walls. Hardin had one time come upon some wormed cedar in the foothills and he had lugged that back in the wagon and made fine panels for the inner bedroom walls. He had been as proud of that as he had been of the hand-split shingles for the roof, and the fireplace he'd mixed up out of adobe mud and straw. And everything now was just as it had been at the time of its beginning; even with Hardin gone. Lupe Varga saw to that. She had a mystic's respect for the wishes of the dead.

When he thought he could manage it Clay pulled himself out of the chair and went toward the doorway. There was one perilous moment when it appeared that Lupe was going to seize him and pour another quart of pinto beans into him, but then she saw the tight ridges which his levis made across his belly and she smiled benevolently and let him proceed.

Efigio came with him to the corral and helped him saddle up. Efigio looked like he might like to come along, but Clay wanted to be alone for awhile and he explained it that way to the Mexican.

"I just want to have a look around," he said. "I ain't rid over our land for I don't know how long and I figure I better get used to it again. I won't be long."

"No? All right, you go, Clay. You go and get it into your insides once more. I stay here and wait for you. Maybe I help Lupe get something ready for dinner."

"Gawdalmighty!" Clay said, and he swung on up.

He rode a long distance that afternoon. He rode until he was aching and sore in nearly every joint and he felt better for it because he was riding across the length and breadth of his own land and there was a point in it.

At last he stopped on a rise a mile or so to the north of the buildings and from there he could see nearly everything that God had made in that great country. A body could stand up there, or sit if he chose, and look and look until he felt no bigger than a grain of sand. He could look way out to the east and see the wide sky bending down to join the unbroken land in a fine, indefinite line. He could see the brown scar the Pecos etched in the earth and the faintly raised ridge of the Mescalero far beyond. He could see forever, and it was only the beginning.

And if seeing all that didn't make him feel humble and small and considerably less important than a lot of people thought they were he could turn his head until he caught the dry wind of Arizona in his nose and see the Guadeloupes and the Sacramentos and the Capitans rearing honest and eternal in the west. Their great shoulders were cloaked in piñon and cedar and great spruce and groves of trembling aspens. Their crags and canyons held more secrets than one could ever hope to learn and a body could only fill himself with a far-off lonesome emptiness when he wondered about them all.

The lonesome emptiness stayed with him to a certain degree when he let his eyes come around and slide along the slope of the rise to the cluster of his buildings down below. For some reason or other his mind had never ventured forward to that time when he would have that place alone; when the responsibility of judgment would be his and when no Hardin would be around to vex with questions and the like. They had built with an attitude of permanence in those early days, and Clay's young mind had been impressed with the notion that the old and comfortable order could never end.

Seeing those buildings lazing in the sun and in the cottonwood shade made him feel a little bit uneasy. He was glad to get home again, but seeing that place all at once the way he was now made him realize the size of the task he was figuring to undertake. It would be enough if everything was proper and in order, but with the help situation as seemingly hopeless as Efigio had pictured it, and with dry-rot and termites and what-not getting ahead of maintenance it would be the kind of uphill hike that might never find the crest.

It made him wonder if a smarter course was not the one which led right on over west there into the mountains. He was pretty well used to that kind of life, the roving kind of life that was to be had over there. It wouldn't be too very hard to pick it up again where he had left it two years and more ago.

He had been up there looking around for twenty minutes or so when the horsemen came into the lane below him and dismounted in the dooryard of the ranch-house. He had been up there, wondering about his uncertain destiny and sending his eyes and thoughts about the land in which he stood. He was particularly looking at the land belonging to Dodge Liston, adjoining his, and away beyond that to a slice of that in John Chisum's name, and seeking in his head to learn just what it was that made some men more greedy in the matter of land than others, when these riders came into the lane and stood down and stretched their arms and legs in the fat shade of the trees.

He rode on down to find out who they were and what was on their minds and he recognized them as he came around the corral and approached them on the Morgan. There were half a dozen of them and he thought how little they had changed since he had seen them last—the Gallagher brothers, Old Man Medford, Jack Harris, Dodge Liston. And one he found he didn't recognize at all. This one still remained upon his horse and rolled a smoke in a casual and somehow disinterested way. He held Clay's attention somewhat more than did the others. Clay had not seen anyone wear his guns lashed down like that since he had run away from Robey Moore.

These men had an uncertain air about them which gave Clay the notion that he was somehow in command of the situation. They had the appearance of men who had come upon a delicate mission and were not exactly certain in what way they were going to broach the matter. Each kept looking at the others, as though hoping someone else would get it going. Only the unknown, of all of them, seemed to know what he was about, and seemed not to give a damn for anything.

"Well," Clay said at last, "I don't expect you came out here just to look at one another like that. What do you want?"

Old Man Medford's wattles moved. "Why, we come out here to welcome you home, Clay, just like good neighbors ought to do. Damned if we didn't."

"That's right," Steve Gallagher said. "We come out here to see how you was, and to see how you was doin' now that you got back from . . . from . . ."

Steve Gallagher looked like he had got an unfamiliar piece of food in his mouth and didn't know just what to do with it. Clay got off a twisted grin and finished the sentence for him. "Prison, Steve. That's where I got back from." He looked them over again and gave the man on the horse a long stare. "I don't think I know you very well," he said.

"Name of Sam Chandler," Dodge Liston said casually. "He's helpin' out with the law around here for a spell." Dodge Liston's round face looked cool and dry in the heat of the day. His clothes were neat and well-cared for and he seemed to get an assurance from them. But Clay could remember when Dodge wasn't different from any other nester.

Clay let his eyes come around to the mounted man again. He had a feeling that he was being sized up by this Chandler person. He had seen men look at him in just that way before and he was reminded somewhat of the impression that Billy Bonney would sometimes make. It made him think that Sam Chandler was likely aware of that himself and no doubt took pleasure in it. There was a lot of gun-hands picking up Bonney's mannerisms now that the Kid was dead.

"Howdy," Clay said. "You find good huntin' with that artillery?"

"Not much yet," Sam Chandler said. "Never can tell, though."

Old Man Medford cleared his throat noisily. "We come to explain that things around these parts have changed, Clay. We're law-abidin' now and we don't have no more shootin' or range wars or no trouble of that sort."

"I'm mighty glad to hear it," Clay said. "Can't get much work done with range wars goin' on. My place, here, is pretty well run to seed 'cause of the last one."

"I was gettin' 'round to that," Old Man Medford said. "Maybe it's so run-down and gone to seed that you was thinkin' of leavin' it altogether. Could be you'd be happier somewhere else."

Clay turned it over in his head and picked up the slant of the conversation. "That could be so," he said. "I guess I ain't been back long enough yet to give it much thought, though."

"The Moore gang's been hanging 'round this country, Forest," Steve Gallagher said, "and we don't like it. We remember you was once a part of that outfit."

"In the Lincoln war, I was," Clay said, "before they went wholly renegade. But that's done. Pa was in it, too. Come to think of it Pa and me was the only ones from here that went into that scrap at all. You might even say that Pa and me fought your battles for you at that time. I don't recall that I saw any of your faces up there on the Hondo or the Bonito or Ruidoso."

Old man Medford took it up again. Old Man Medford had thick blue veins in the fat of his neck and they bulged when he got excited or disturbed. "That ain't neither here nor there, Forest," he said. "We're just sayin' the Moore gang's still workin', and for all we know you may be, too."

Clay leaned against the tie-rail and eyed Sam Chandler. Sam Chandler's hands drifted to his belt line. "Maybe it's time you people took off," Clay said. "I had a hard day and I aim to turn in early. I ain't much for talkin' just now."

"Maybe you're somethin' for thinkin', then," Steve Gallagher said. "Might be good for you to do some of that."

They mounted up and rode off, but Dodge Liston lingered.

"They mean business, Clay," he said. "There's a new situation in this valley. The Santa Fe's come down through Raton to Lamy and Albuquerque and she's goin' straight on out to California. And she's goin' to come down in here, too. This is gettin' to be civilized country. They aim to make it that way."

"Where do you stand, Dodge?" Clay said. "Seems to me you rode in here with 'em."

"I ain't maybe so hard as them, Clay. If you was choosin' to leave I might be able to give you a decent price."

"What kind of a price would that be, Dodge?"

Dodge Liston ran his hand along his smoothly shaven face. "Well, I'd have to figure some on that. 'Course this here spread ain't near as good as it used to be, now, Clay. She's run down pretty bad and I hear a good deal of your beef wandered off while you was away. Them buildings, too, they'd need some attention; a lot of it. Might even be best to tear 'em down altogether and start new."

Clay rocked back on his heels and listened to Dodge Liston talk. It was almost a pleasure to hear a man carry on like that. Dodge never blowed hard and loud like Old Man Medford or the Gallaghers. He just flowed along smooth and easy, and he was more the dangerous because of it.

"I don't suppose the railroad comin' through here—if it ever does—would make much difference, would it?" Clay said. "They might even have to lay some track across my land. But, that wouldn't enter into your figurin', now, would it, Dodge?"

The sun was not on Dodge Liston's face, but it was colored up like it anyway. "I wouldn't know nothin' about what the railroad's goin' to do," he said. "I'm just tryin' to do you a favor, that's all."

Dodge caught up the reins of his bridle and heaved himself into the saddle. He sat square and solid and looked down at Clay. "I expect it'd do you some good to think it over."

"I expect it would," Clay said. "And in the meantime I'm goin' to get me some help out here and get the place in shape."

Dodge picked at the mane of his horse and smiled. "Kind of odd about that," he said. "All the spreads hereabouts has been hirin' like crazy lately. Ain't much help to be found at any price."

"Like that, huh?"

"Like that, Clay, just like that."

Dodge swung his horse around and headed down the lane of cottonwoods, and Clay stood there and watched the shadows of the branches make their curious patterns across his back. Some of those trees had been planted by Hardin, but others were as old as any man around there could recall. Their roots were deep and they held memories.

Efigio came out as Dodge Liston passed beyond the last of them and out of sight.

"I see you riding before," he said, "and I wonder what you think. You maybe have it in your head to leave this place."

Clay stared down the cottonwood canyon, watching the old ghosts move among the trunks. "Yeah, I guess I did," he said. "I'm figurin' to stay, though, after all. Them trees are sure pretty ain't they?"

"Sí," Efigio said. "Sí, they are life itself."

• CHAPTER 4 •
The Hard Way

THEY WORKED HARD IN THOSE DAYS AND THERE NEVER seemed an end to it. It made no difference what time of the early morning they rolled out; they were never finished with what they had to do when day was ended. Sundown always found the work piled as high and endless as the day before and it sometimes seemed that death itself would bring their only respite.

Efigio was uncomplaining in the saddle but he would agonize like a Penitente in his morada when it came to work around the casa and the other buildings. He did not seem to mind having reins or a quirt in his hand for endless hours, or even days, but when his fingers found themselves around a hammer or a saw he was very likely apt to be overcome with fatigue and lassitude. He could not stand a thing like that for long, and was always seeking causes to be sent out on the range again.

Clay knew he needed help, and badly. The two of

them could not hope to get that place in shape and run it properly. There was too much to do for two men; it required the greatest kind of effort of both of them, and still it got ahead of them. He took to riding into town to see what he could find. Only a few trips, though, told him it was pretty much as Dodge had prophesied. Every able hand had long since been signed up by other outfits and Clay had no wish to cull the saloons for the dregs that might be found in them. One or two of that stripe might not be bad if he could watch them all the time, but a thing like that was out of the question and he had to have those who would accept responsibility and do their work without an eye upon their backs.

He got help in an unexpected manner. He came upon it in town, and he stuck pretty close to home. There was nothing to be found down there in that huddle of planked and adobe buildings sprawled along the Pecos; and anyway, he did not like the way that the people in that place would look at him. They made him think of those evil-lookers who had greeted his first day of freedom up in Vegas. They made him think of Robey, and tended to keep his association with that man fresh and poignant in his mind. They would not let him forget that he had been sent to prison for an act of murder.

So he stayed close to home.

He did most of the repair work on the buildings and the fences, but sometimes he would weary of that and ride on out and breathe the clean, dry wind carrying along the sweep of land that was his range. One day he walked the Morgan out beyond the rise to the north and when he crossed the crest and paused to look around he saw the rider working up the other side, coming in a long slant from the Pecos boundary of his land.

Clay backed off the crest, swung down and pulled his Winchester from the saddle scabbard. He lay down behind a growth of yucca and watched this man come up the slope. He was coming slowly and taking his time and stopping every now and then to hike up in his stirrups and take a look around him. It did not seem to Clay that he was on a peaceful mission.

He was pretty close when he got down and hunched up the slope to get an eye on the buildings far down on the other side. Clay could see that this man was young, boy-like almost, and that he was humping up the rise in a manner that betokened wariness and a certain caution, as though he was not exactly sure of what it was that he was about. He had left his rifle in its scabbard.

Clay waited for him to get settled in the grass before he moved. Then he slipped over the rise and worked down to where he could get behind the other. As he came near to the horse he squatted quiet for a moment and studied it. The animal was a tough little cattle-working mustang with clean, hardy lines. It wore a plain, neat saddle with a minimum of decoration, and there was an air of competence about the other gear upon it. It made him think that its rider might be a good hand when it came to handling beef. But the flank of that horse was etched deep in Old Man Medford's brand.

Clay edged up the slope directly to the rear of the man lying belly-down in the grass. When he got fifteen yards away he knew he was a youngster. He had removed his hat and was reclining with his chin upon his crossed arms in front of him. There were big, red freckles on the one cheek that Clay could see, and his hair was a crazy smash of rust on his head. His gun was down along his hip and there wasn't much that he could do when Clay kneed up and took the rifle into both his hands.

"Howdy," Clay said to him, "you lookin' for me?"

The youngster turned around slow-like and put his hands up.

"Clay," he said. "Clay Forest. Mister Clay Forest."

"You hit it right three times," Clay said. "What you doin' up here?"

I'm just lookin', Mister Forest, that's all. I was just lookin' at your buildings down there. Little old Clint Rhodes was just takin' a pasear over here to have a look."

Clay felt a grin tugging at the corner of his mouth. "So I see," he said. "I been watchin' you for fifteen minutes. Seems to me you could have been more careful."

"I didn't come to do no harm," Clint Rhodes said. "Otherwise, I would have been."

"You're another one I ain't seen around these parts before," Clay said to him.

"Ain't been here but three years. Came on out after my pa was killed in a stampede near Abilene. Never did have no ma that I knew of. I'm on my own, have been since I was sixteen."

"Kind of a maverick, ain't you?" Clay said.

"Yes, sir, I guess I am. I know how to work, though. I been makin' my own way for a spell. Just now lookin' at your spread down there; I figure I could put my hand to shorin' up them saggin' buildin's, square up them old shingles, and mend them fences proper."

Clay had a hard time with his grin. "That horse you got's wearin' old Man Medford's brand."

"I know," Clint Rhodes said. "And I'm goin' to miss him. He's a world-beater certain. Ain't many can stick with a steer like him. Almost dogs him down by hisself."

"Ain't you happy with Old Man Medford?"

"No, I guess I ain't. I don't like the way they talk over there. I came over here to see if you was as bad as some of them say you are. Don't seem that you could be, but I had to find out."

Clay put the Winchester in his lap when he sat down. Clint Rhodes' smile split his face clean across in big, yellow teeth, and he rubbed his arms.

"I ain't so bad," Clay said. "They just got ideas about me, that's all. They figure 'cause me and Pa fought in the Lincoln war that we is a smirch on the fair name of this here valley. We had a notion that we was doin' right, though."

"Uh-huh, I tried to get into it, too, but there wasn't nobody'd sign me on. I'd just got out here then and they all said I was too much of a kid."

Clay worked up a cigarette and lit it. "Who would you have sided?"

"I figured I'd 'ave sided McSween's bunch—them as was avengin' Tunstall. Only I never got to do it."

"I guess maybe we'd 'o seen eye to eye in that, then," Clay said. "You'd of maybe been unpopular with some, though."

"I more or less worked that out for myself," Clint Rhodes said. "Most others here said it was bad to take sides in a big thing like that—with gunslicks up from Mexico and all. They said only fools'd ride into that."

"Yeah, I remember people sayin' things like that at the time."

"I guess maybe that's why I got curious about you," Clint Rhodes said. "That's why I came up here when I heard you was back."

"You figure you're satisfied now?"

"Nope, I reckon I'm still curious."

"This can likely shape up into something big," Clay said. "I already had all kinds of invitations to leave again."

"I know about that, too. It don't make no difference."

Clay stood up and squashed the cigarette under

his heel. "I guess we'd best get on down to the house, then. Bring your horse along and we'll get him back to Medford somehow. We got some pretty fair ones on our string."

"All right. I'd like to keep him, but I don't guess that's the best thing, is it?"

"No, we'll likely have enough on our hands without somebody else's horse, too. You know this Sam Chandler?"

"Uh-huh. They got him up here as a kind of marshal. I guess he works for everybody. They say he's a pretty handy feller; I can't say for certain, though."

"Yeah, well, we'll think about that when we come to it."

They walked on down the rise to get Clint's horse, then went back up on the long slant toward the Morgan. Driving his legs up that slope made Clay aware of the gnawing in his belly, and he remembered that he hadn't eaten in several hours.

"Say," he said. "You hungry?"

Clint Rhodes laughed. "I surely am. Seems I ain't et nothin' in a week. I guess that stalkin' around gets a feller's appetite up."

Clay chuckled to himself as they came across the crest. "Lupe's goin' to like this," he said. "This is goin' to be a holiday for her."

Clint Rhodes was a hard and willing worker. He was smart with a saw and hammer and he had a good, strong back for lifting. He was a great joy to Efigio because of this, and his appetite was a source of endless delight for Lupe. He fit into things around there pretty well; and one day he did a thing which won him Clay's unceasing admiration.

Most of the time Clint stayed around the ranch, doing the things that had to be done to make them stand up straight, but Clay knew that too much of that was no good for any buckaroo, and he would on occasion send him out to ride awhile. One of these times he rode on out and he had not been gone for more than twenty minutes before gunfire broke across the rise and filled the dooryard with its distant sound.

It brought Clay and Efigio on a dead run for their horses, but they had barely cleared the corral and headed for the rise when Clint appeared. He had a stranger fastened to the front sight of his Winchester. This stranger was walking along and Clint was leading his horse behind his own. They were still far off, but Clay recognized him anyway. Only one man had a shambling walk like that. It was Diamond-Back, right hand man for Robey Moore.

It was Clint's show and Clay let him herd Diamond-Back into the dooryard before he got into it himself. He knew that Diamond-Back was not accustomed to walking for great distances and he could tell that he was not taking kindly to the treatment. His lean, hungry face was set in sullenness and his long arms flapped belligerently at his sides. He was in a sour mood. Clay's laughter did not seem to improve it any.

"What'd you expect?" Clay said to him. "Can't nobody come prowlin' 'round without they're goin' to attract attention."

"I was doin' nothin' whatsoever," Diamond-Back said. "I was simply comin' peaceful-like to see you, when this half-grown punk like to cut me down."

"He was up behind the rise, there," Clint Rhodes said. "He was sneakin' through the grass with his rifle just like a snake of some kind. I thought best to shoot that out of his hands and talk about it later."

"I was just lookin' to see if it was clear, that's all."

"That's where he gets his name," Clay said. "Diamond-Back; kind of a snake-like feller at that, when you come to think of it."

Diamond-Back glared around him. "Pretty smart-talkin', ain't you? I seen the day when you wasn't so wise, Forest. I seen the day when you didn't know your right hand from your left."

"Most everyone grows up and learns," Clay said. "Some don't though. Some just keep on and never learn nothin' at all. Them's the kind that generally comes in at gunpoint."

Diamond-Back spat in the dry dust at his feet. "Talk's cheap, Forest. Don't cost nothin' when you got the high hand."

Clay fished his paper and tobacco from his pocket. He poured some for himself, then passed the stuff around. Everyone but Diamond-Back built one up.

"Don't smoke no more?" Clay said to him.

"Depends on the company," Diamond-Back said.

Clay lit up and threw the match away. "All right, now, what you doin' here?"

Diamond-Back got some of his assurance back. "Robey wants you," he said. He appeared to take strength and swagger from the mention of that name and he stuck his thumbs in his gunbelt and smiled around. "He says you better get humpin' for the hills; he's been expectin' you. You made him unhappy by not showin' soon's you got out. That's why he sent me down."

"I guess he's goin' to remain unhappy, then," Clay said. "You can go on back and tell him so. I already told him where I stood one time before, but maybe he didn't think I meant it."

"Ain't nobody leaves Robey permanent 'less they're dead," Diamond-Back said. "You got signs of life."

"Well, I'm one that did. Granted, I done it the hard way, but I done it anyway. He's got no complaint on what I done. I stuck with him through the most of the scrappin'. But I don't put up with that other stuff. I ain't no wanton killer."

Diamond-Back worked up another smile. "I heard a jury said different a couple years back."

"Jury's been wrong before, and likely will be again. No way to find a dozen impartial men in the middle of a cattle war. Anyway, that's aside the point. I ain't comin' back to Robey and you can tell him so. If he wants to go into the matter further he can come down himself. Now, you can go."

"I ain't in no hurry," Diamond-Back said.

Clint Rhodes pushed the rifle into Diamond-Back. "You heard the boss, mister. Get on this hoss."

Diamond-Back's face got red and ugly, but he complied. He swung on up and sat in a mean hunk in the saddle. His face reflected the pale, yellow cast of his eyes when he looked at Clint.

"I got a good mind for faces," he said. "I ain't likely to forget yours right off."

"I got a good nose for smells, myself," Clint Rhodes said. "I'll know when you're around."

"All right, now, git," Clay said. He hauled back and brought the dust jumping out of the flank of Diamond-Back's horse with the flat of his hand, and the horse surged, startled. It ran ahead for five yards before Diamond-Back got it under hand, and the gunslick kept it moving. They were a hundred yards away before anyone spoke again.

"I seen that brand," Clint Rhodes said then. "It's Dodge Liston's. And he come right over here with it."

"Yeah, Diamond-Back don't give a damn for nothin'," Clay said. "Old Man Medford had it straight. Robey's workin' this valley, all right."

And he now had himself a notion why.

• CHAPTER 5 •
Bullet Barricade

He COULD NOT GET DIAMOND-BACK OUT OF HIS MIND.
Diamond-Back was in his head like one of those old
ballads which Efigio would sometimes sing and
which would jump around in his thinking for days
on end and wouldn't leave for anything. Coming back
home to this valley, he'd thought he'd had everything
like that pretty well under control, but now he found
he hadn't. Diamond-Back stayed back in there and
watched him, his cold, yellow eyes blinking out of
his lean face. Diamond-Back, and yes, Robey and Ed
Picket and Bob Fergus and Steve Howard. The term
in prison had made them seem another lifetime and
a million miles away, but Diamond-Back's showing
up like that had changed it all again. They were as
near and close as they'd ever been. They were just
over yonder, watching; watching, and maybe waiting
for a chance of some kind.

Altogether, Clay was with Robey Moore for the
best part of a year. They lived mostly in the hills and

deep timber up around Lincoln, in the ranch houses of friends, isolated cabins, though they occasionally spent time in a kind of barracks McSween had rigged up in the store building he partnered with Tunstall in Lincoln.

They were outdoor men, though, and it was better in the hills and forests. After Sheriff Brady had been gunned down by Billy Bonney the streets of Lincoln were risky ground for the anti-Murphy forces anyway—Brady being a Murphy man—so it was just as well. The timber and mountains around there were nice for Clay, though they seemed possessed of a greater and more awesome magnificence than those that he remembered in Kentucky. But they were partly spoiled for him by the killing of Buckshot Roberts. When that happened the Lincoln fight commenced to have a bad taste in the mouth for him. It made him see that Robey was in it simply for the killings to be had. It caused him to wonder if he had not stayed with that bunch too long. It was the thing which finally drove him to make his break. He had followed Hardin's admonition as far as his conscience would let him go.

Nobody seemed to know just why they were going up to Blazer's Mill that day to meet Dick Brewer. If Robey knew he said nothing and the rest of them had learned that it did not always pay to bother Moore with questions. They had gotten used to being ruled with an iron hand.

"Brewer's got himself a constable's badge from Justice of the Peace Wilson and he's taking a posse to Blazer's and we're going to meet him there," was about all Robey said and he left it at that. The rest of them could only wonder about it as they rode along.

"Maybe Murphy's got him a big bunch together up there and Brewer and Robey got wind of it," Ed Picket said.

"What business would he have at Blazer's Mill?" Clay said. "The Indian Agency's on that land and it's government property. It don't seem right that he'd risk a fight there."

"Maybe there ain't goin' to be no fight." Steve Howard said. "Brewer's got him a badge, ain't he?"

"Everybody gets a badge when they want one," Clay said. "It don't make no difference what side they're on. Everybody figures what he's doin' is right and just, and likes to have some sign of it."

"Well, anyway, we don't know nothin'," Steve Howard said. "Likely ain't goin' to be no fight at all."

"I didn't say there was goin' to be," Clay said. "I just said it don't seem like good sense for Murphy to make a stand on that ground. He'd be mixin' real trouble, then."

Diamond-Back came up beside them in a widening of the trail. "Feller named Buckshot Roberts hangs around up in there; it's my guess that's got somethin' to do with it."

Clay turned it over in his mind; it was a name he'd heard only a few times, and did not associate it with the fighting in the past.

"Who's he?" he said. "Who's this Buckshot Roberts?"

Diamond-Back smiled into the screen of cedar along the trail. "Just an old goat who figures he don't have to take sides in this business; he ain't yet learned he can't stay neutral."

"How can Brewer expect to arrest him for that?" Clay said. "That ain't no crime."

"It depends on how you look at it," Diamond-Back said. "This Roberts is an old Indian-fighter. He's got enough lead in him to start his own shot foundry. They say he can't even lift his arms for the dead weight of 'em. He's settin' a bad example."

"How so is that?" Clay said. "Don't sound to me

like he could fight even if he wanted to. What's wrong with his stayin' out of it?"

"He's loud," Diamond-Back said. "Fellers say he makes too much talk that don't sound right."

"And Brewer thinks he can arrest him for a thing like that?" Clay said.

Diamond-Back shrugged, and that seemed to end it.

They kept on riding. Clay rode nearly behind Robey and he kept his eyes on the leader. That Robey surely sat his horse in an informed manner. Lots of fellers were pretty good at that but they still left the impression of being conscious of what they were doing; but not Robey. He rode like his horse was a part of him. Like it was maybe a leg or an arm that would do exactly what he'd planned for it to do without any real thinking on it or conscious guiding of it. That was the way that he did everything. Like he knew far in advance just exactly what was going to happen, and had already put his mind ahead to something else.

Buckshot Roberts stayed in Clay's mind. "You don't figure all those people are goin' to scrap it up with just that one old cripple, do you?" he said to Diamond-Back after awhile.

"I don't know nothin'," Diamond-Back said. "But what if they do? Feller's got to have some shootin' now and then. Else he goes stale."

It was too important to Clay to let it set there and he pushed the Morgan up to range with Robey Moore. Moore had his empty eyes off in the brush somewhere and it was a minute or so before he seemed to be aware of Clay.

"There's talk we're goin' up there to see about an old cripple," Clay said then. "This Buckshot Roberts that don't choose sides with no one."

When Robey looked at a man that man felt like he

was naked and there wasn't nothing he could hide. Clay got to picking at a seam in his pants.

"Fellers ain't happy 'less they talk," Robey said. "And the less they know the more they talk. Human nature, I reckon."

"Well, is it true, or ain't it?" Clay said. "Don't seem right to trouble an old guy like that 'cause he's got his mind set in a manner that don't please everyone else."

"Well, you don't want to bother your head about any trouble he might have," Robey said. "You was comin' along pretty well, and now you get nosey again. I thought we understood one another."

"I reckon we do," Clay said. "But I don't hold with a thing like this. Might be all right for Brewer to take him in, if'n he'll go, but he don't sound like the sort that will. That means fightin' and I ain't about to draw down on no old cripple."

Robey took a long time thinking that one over. It seemed to Clay that he'd never speak again. Then he said, "You ain't, huh."

Clay knew they'd reached some kind of impasse, but he'd found his ground and he was standing on it. He'd never done a thing to be ashamed of and he wasn't going to start with Robey Moore.

"No, I ain't," he said; and he looked straight at Robey when he said it.

He saw the beginning of it when they came through the trees and approached Doc Blazer's Mill. He saw this old guy, who must be Buckshot Roberts, standing in the doorway and making talk with the riders drawn up there in the clearing before the building. He held a rifle loosely in his hands as though he maybe had an intimation of what was going to happen. There were hard men in that company and their intentions were not artfully concealed.

Clay saw Buckshot making wary conversation with

Dick Brewer. Beside Brewer there were ten or a dozen other men. They were mostly men that he knew and there were a few with whom he'd basked around a campfire, or maybe split a shank of venison with; the Coe brothers, Doc Skurlock the gambler from Lincoln, John Middleton, Tom O'Folliard, Jake Scoggins, Jim French, Charlie Bowdre, Frank McNab and a few others he did not know by name. William Bonney was with them, too.

The shooting started before Robey's bunch got to the building. It broke out when Charlie Bowdre fired point blank from the hip and sent a slug through Buckshot's body. Clay saw the small puff of dust burst out from Buckshot's clothing, and he saw him return the fire with the rifle before he staggered inward and slammed the door. After that it was a state of siege.

Everybody made for the brush and cover. Clay took the Morgan back in deep and staked him out with his reata. He had a sick, weak feeling inside his middle. He tried to think that this thing was not real, but he knew it was. It was happening and he was in it. He had a notion to mount up and run right then, but he knew he couldn't yet. Robey Moore was there to see to that.

"You come with me, Forest," he said. "We're spreadin' out in these trees here, and you come with me. I aim to see you get some good, clean shootin'."

Clay went. He left the Winchester in the scabbard and hoped Robey wouldn't notice it. The Colt was enough for the shooting he felt he was going to do. Those fat, old slugs wouldn't pierce through the way the rifle's would. He just hoped Buckshot would keep down and out of sight.

They went through the trees and bellied down behind a slight lift in the ground. When they could view the building again Clay saw that Buckshot had gotten in some licks. He saw George Coe running through the trees with his hand streaming blood, one finger missing. He saw John Middleton walking along there in the open like he had no particular place to go and didn't know from where he'd started. There was a big, red splotch on his shirt and blood was coming out of his mouth. He coughed and little bubbles formed around his lips. He barely made cover before he fell over in a heap.

Robey Moore commenced to lever brass from behind the lift. Buckshot could not be seen, but Robey was sending lead into the building anyway. Watching him, Clay saw his face lying hard and tanned against the rife stock. There was a soft turn to his lips as though there was nothing else he'd rather do. Clay wondered how a man could get that way; how a man could kill another man for pleasure, just like shooting pigeons in the trees.

The sun went higher and the siege dragged on. They'd been there for hours and hadn't much to show for it. Roberts was hurt bad, likely dying slow in there, but he was fighting still. He'd got some arnament in there and a mixture of fire was coming from the building. Most of it was small arms now, but now and then Clay would hear the big boom of an old Sharps buffalo gun. He kept hoping Roberts would connect with that.

He could tell that everyone was getting fidgety and impatient. Over a bit, he saw Dick Brewer talking it over with Scoggins and McNab and he knew they were getting tired of it. Pretty soon Brewer backed away and sneaked over under cover of the trees. He dipped his hand at Clay and Robey as he passed in back of them.

"I'm goin' to get that big bag of wind," he said. "He's doin' too much damage; he's gettin' to think he owns the place."

Clay watched him edge away and when he saw him

again he was down the line some behind a pile of logs. He was shielded from the building but Clay could see him fine. He could see the window from which Roberts was firing, too, and he had the feeling that something was going to come of this. It'd gone on too long and something was bound to break.

A kind of quiet had come over the fighting and Clay knew that everyone was waiting. He kept on watching Brewer, and Buckshot's window, and he didn't care if Robey had his eyes on him or not. He knew his yearning for Roberts was showing in his face, but it didn't make any difference anymore.

When Brewer opened fire Buckshot returned it, but nothing came of the first exchange. Brewer was too far down for Buckshot to get a bead on him, and he was maybe too far down to get himself a bead on Buckshot, because he bellied up the pile some for the next one. That he chopped a whisk of chips away from the windowsill, and when Buckshot got his gun out again Clay saw it was the Sharps. He took a long time in his sighting, but when he squeezed the trigger it was worth it. The big gob of lead took the top of Brewer's head off. The shooting all around picked up again and Clay got the new feeling in him. He knew what he was going to do. He pulled the Colt around and pushed it into Robey's ribs. Robey looked at him as though he'd never set his eyes on him before.

"Come on with me," Clay said. "Let the rifle lie right there and come with me."

Robey made a blind move as though to swing the Winchester around and Clay chopped at his arm with the Colt. "I said to leave it. Leave it right there, and move."

Clay backed off into the brush and Robey came with him. Robey was beginning to smile now, as though there was a quality of humor in the incident which had just occurred to him. He didn't even lose it when Clay took his Colt away from him. It made Clay nervous and jumpy all over again and he had the notion that Robey was just as dangerous unarmed as the other way around.

He prodded Robey through the trees and toward the staked out Morgan. They were going quietly but there was gunfire racketing around in there anyway and it didn't make much difference. Clay's fear was the chance of being spotted by someone lying in the brush, but it didn't happen and he got the reata coiled and hung without any trouble. He mounted up and looked at Robey's smiling face.

"So long, Robey," he said. "I rode with you like Pa said to do but I don't hold with this. I'm finished now. I done my part."

Robey's expression hadn't changed at all. "So long, Forest," he said. "I'll see you around some day. I'll look you up. I'll find you. You're mine, kid. You belong to me."

"No, I don't," Clay said. "I belong to myself."

But they were both wrong, at least for a time, and Clay always remembered the irony of it. For the next two years Clay was a possession of the existing government.

• CHAPTER 6 •
Honor-Bound

AFTER CLINT RHODES HAD BROUGHT DIAMOND-BACK IN that way Clay could not keep his mind from going back to all those things again. For a number of days after Diamond-Back had gone away, that business up at Blazer's Mill was in his head as strongly as the day it had occurred. He kept remembering what Robey had said to him when he had finally made his break. He was not afraid of Robey but Diamond-Back's appearance had filled him with a sense of urgency. He felt the shadows of his past seeping down upon him from the humped hills over west. He knew something was going to happen soon.

He took to riding his range more than he had been doing before. He and Clint and Efigio ran token tallies on the herd from time to time. He did not think seriously that Robey would take the trouble to make a pass at it, but, still, with Robey a body wasn't sure. The feeling persisted in him that Robey and the old bunch were out there somewhere, keeping their eyes on him.

One day he ran into Dodge Liston out on his land, and his estimation of that person's capabilities increased. From a long way off he saw him crossing over from his own line, and he ducked down into an arroyo to see what he was going to do.

It was hot down in that place and he was uncomfortable. The sun beat down upon him like a metal mallet and the dust stirred up by the Morgan's hooves did not settle and carry off in the windless air. There were prickly pear and sand burrs to add to his discomfiture. But he stayed down in there anyway.

This slit in the baked earth was narrow but maybe a quarter of a mile in length. He had entered at the southern end of it, dismounted and crept up the sloping side to have a look around. He saw Dodge coming easily and taking his time. If he had any notions he was being watched he did not show it, and he did not seem to care. He rode in the wide open like that for quite awhile. Now and then he would draw up or take a cut to one side of his general line of travel as though he might be looking for some sign. It seemed like he had all day to spend out there. Finally, a row of hummocks intervened, and Clay slid down the slope and walked further up the cut.

When he climbed up for another look around, Dodge Liston had disappeared. Clay had a more commanding view from this place than he had had before, but that made no difference whatsoever. The other man was as completely gone as if he'd never been out there in the first place. It filled Clay with a feeling of bafflement and slowly growing wonder. The thought that a man could evade his eyes like that was not appealing.

When he turned to slide back down again he saw Dodge watching him. Dodge had gotten around to the other side of the arroyo and was sitting his horse in a negligent manner and seeming to take an enjoyment in the proceedings down below. Having failed to watch his rear as he should have made Clay feel like a fool. And Dodge's subtle turning of his flank that way made him regard the other man with a new-found feeling of respect. He had learned a valuable thing and he appreciated it.

"You lose something down there, Clay?" Dodge Liston asked him. "Don't see a man'd wallow around in the heat of a ditch like that 'less he was lookin' for somethin'."

Clay slapped the alkali out of his shirt and pants and mounted the Morgan, which had trailed him down the draw. They went in switchbacks to the top before he answered. He felt awkward, as though he was guilty of some minor indiscretion; like maybe taking melons when he hadn't ought to.

"I might ask you the same thing," he said when he sat up on top again. "I might ask you what you was doin' over here when you got all that land of your own to ride around on."

He felt angry and he didn't care just how he sounded. Dodge was sitting there cool and composed and had him at a disadvantage.

"I guess I was lookin' for somethin' at that," Dodge said. "I was lookin' for a horse. One of my waddies said he saw one of my string over this way a few days back. It had a man upon it." Clay remembered Diamond-Back again. It made him swear deep down inside him, but that did not help at all.

"I ain't got no horse of yours," he said. "Only horse been around here that ain't mine was one belongin' to Old Man Medford. Clint Rhodes rode him over and we sent him back."

He did not know why he felt compelled to explain about Old Man Medford's horse, and it made him boil inside to do it. But Dodge had got him on the defensive and there was no helping it.

"Feller that seen this horse of mine said also that this rider looked mighty familiar to him," Dodge went on. "Said he looked like one of the old Moore bunch. Fact is, this waddie of mine is set to swear on the biggest Bible in the Pecos Valley that this rider was a man called Diamond-Back."

Clay had got a grip on himself. "Well, now, that could be," he said, "only I don't think so, 'cause I know about nearly everything that comes by here. Anyway, Diamond-Back's doin's ain't no affair of mine. I ain't had no truck with that outfit since the Lincoln war. Had no part in all their depredations. Diamond-Back might be dead for all I know. Lot of fellers got killed up there, you know."

"I suppose it could have been his ghost, then," Dodge said. "But he surely had an eye for horse-flesh. That cayuse was one of my very best. I surely miss him."

That time Clay got a chuckle out. He saw the humor in it, then, "Yeah, it could have been his ghost," he said. "I always remembered Diamond-Back as bein' choosey 'bout his horses when he was alive."

They rode on leg and leg, down toward the ranch, and Dodge appeared to have forgotten about his missing horse for the moment, but Clay knew he hadn't done anything like that at all. He knew Dodge was playing a waiting game.

"I expect you've been doin' some thinkin', Clay," Dodge said after a bit. "You been considerin' what you and me talked about before?"

"Been a little busy around here to think much, Dodge. Takes a lot of time to work this place and there ain't much left for thinkin' 'bout anything like that."

"I expect not; not without help. You don't want to take too long, though."

"I got help, now," Clay said. "Clint Rhodes is with me."

"Old Man Medford was talkin' 'bout that the other day. Said Clint never could pull his share of the load."

"He's pullin' it for me, Dodge. I expect it's in the spirit."

Dodge Liston turned his big bulk in the saddle. "Listen, Clay, I ain't goin' to fool around with this forever. Others around here are a blamed sight more het up about my horse goin' off than I am. They don't like the idea of Moore's man takin' it in broad daylight and then comin' over on your land. They ain't so sure that you didn't maybe know about it all the time."

"If they're thinkin' that, then let 'em come around and say it. What do you think, Dodge?"

They had come to a level place a half mile or so above Clay's buildings and Clay could see the small activity going around down there. A cook fire was breathing its slight smoke through the kitchen chimney and a hammer's beat made a soft, thick sound of hominess. On the grey ranch roof, Clint's new shingles stood out like freshly-minted pennies in a handful of old coins.

"I think you better pay more attention to what I've said to you, Clay . . . one of these days a bunch is liable to ride out here and take you in tow. I'm offerin' to help you salvage somethin' from this mess o' yours, and you'd better listen to it."

"You figure they'd do a thing like that?" Clay said.

"I wouldn't put it past 'em," Dodge Liston said.

"I guess, then, I'll have to put you off again, Dodge," Clay said. "Your sayin' that changed it all. I feel honor-bound to stick around long enough to see a thing like that."

Dodge rode off with his back straight and his neck red under the brim of his hat. Clay took the Morgan down to the ranch and turned him into the corral. Coming around to the dooryard, he saw Lupe standing with her hands bundled into her apron, and Efigio and Clint talking to a man sitting on a tall, bay horse. This man sat easy and careless-like and Clay saw Chandler's face beneath the hat. Clay felt the don't-give-a-damn exuding from Chandler as he came across the yard toward him.

"A great day for callers," Clay said. "Seems lots of folks took a notion to come over here today."

"Chandler, here, says he wanted to see you," Clint Rhodes said. "I asked him what he wanted, but he wouldn't say. Wouldn't talk to us about it."

Efigio bored a hole in the earth with the toe of his boot. "He no say nothing. He sit there like a bulto and we look at one another. I think we maybe drive him off, but then we see you coming."

Chandler's lips were curved and it irritated Clay. Chandler was sitting there and watching them as though he maybe owned the place.

"Well," Clay said. "I'm here. What the devil do you want?"

"I come to talk to you about a running iron," Sam Chandler said. "There was one picked up over at the Gallaghers'. I was curious to know if you had any idea as to who might be swingin' a long rope in these parts."

"Seems to me you ought to know more about that than me," Clay said. "You're the only one around here I know of that appears to have the time to stick his nose into other people's business."

Sam Chandler turned his head and watched the cottonwoods wave their heads against the sky. The wind blew soft up there among the crowns, but it was still and quiet in the dooryard.

"When they found this thing they ran a quick talley and figured there was maybe fifty to a hundred

head not accounted for. All prime stock. No year-
lings bothered. Likely countin' on a quick turnover."

"I wouldn't know just how rustlers worked," Clay
said. "If it was me, now, I'd likely run the calves off.
I like the taste of liver."

"Now, that's a funny thing," Sam Chandler said.
" 'Cause the brand they found was yours." Chandler
reached beneath the saddle blanket on the far side
and tossed the short, iron rod down to Clay, who
caught it. "Here, I brung it back to you. Kind of a
waste to leave it lyin' out like that."

Clay turned the brand in his hands. It was the pine-
tree brand, all right, just like Pa had fashioned it
from remembrance of the big trees back there in the
soft Kentucky hills. But the hammer-work wasn't
his. Clay kept watching Chandler when he passed
the iron to Efigio.

"This yours, Efigio?"

Efigio considered it. "No, Clay, it is not mine. I
have never make them like this. I like to have a nice
handle on the ones I make. Yes, a nice handle is a
very important thing."

"I guess that's the answer, Chandler," Clay said.
"This thing don't belong here. I guess some blacksmith was havin' him some practice."

"Could be it wasn't just a blacksmith," Chandler
said. Chandler was talking careful now, and not sitting up there with so much swagger.

"You better git," Clay said. "I'm tired of seein'
your face around here. I don't think you better come
back again."

Sam Chandler eased his horse around. "Maybe I
won't have no choice about it, Forest. Folks hereabouts don't like the way things seem to be stirrin'
since you got back."

"Let 'em move on out, then," Clay said. "There's
big land out here and a lot of sky above it. Me, I'm
stayin' on. I like it here."

"Maybe you are," Chandler said, and he nudged the belly of the bay. "And then again, maybe you ain't."

Clay held the iron in his hand and watched Sam Chandler go on down the cottonwood alley. He had a nice sit to him and it made Clay remember the way that Robey Moore rode. He looked at the rod once more, turning it slowly in the palm of his hand. It wasn't bad work, but it wasn't Pa's.

"Damn Robey," he said.

"Oh-ho," Efigio said quietly. "That is it."

Clay moved his head and looked away on off at the western hills, lounging like big fat shadows on the far horizon. "Yeah, it's Robey, all right. I reckon Diamond-Back wasn't foolin'. I guess I got somethin' on my hands, now."

"Make it 'we,' " Clint Rhodes said.

Somehow, that made Clay feel better.

· CHAPTER 7 ·
Gunman's Score

THAT WAS THE BEGINNING OF IT. THE HORSE THAT Diamond-Back had taken, and then the iron. Or maybe they were simply the first things which seemed to point a finger of definite guilt at the ranch in the shadows of the cottonwood lane. Clay had known from talk around that Robey was giving the neighborhood his attention, but now he was certain he was working it with a purpose. He remembered that Robey was never one to be denied for long the things which he considered to be his.

Examples of this came with freshness to his mind. He recalled a Spanish girl that Robey had one time taken a fancy to. Her old man had kept a herd of sheep and they had lived together in the foothills of the Capitans, not far from Encinosa. This girl, whose name Clay could no longer recall, viewed Robey's interest with enthusiasm, a thing not shared by her old man. And in that Spanish household the father's word was law.

His objections did not sit well with Robey Moore. It might have been a simple matter for him to induce the sloe-eyed girl to ride out with him and to hell with her old man, but Robey's mind was accustomed to following more devious paths. He was out to make that herder eat his words.

Among the accoutrements of his trade, Robey possessed a Bowie knife of singular edge and beauty. He would sometimes sit before an evening campfire and hone it on his boot-sole by the hour. One night he took that knife and crept in amongst the Spanish father's sheep. He cut the life from eleven of those woolly throats. The next night he made mutton of half a dozen more. He kept at it for a week and in the end he got the Spanish father's blessing. He got the girl as well, for all the good it did him. Four days later she was shot from the saddle in a running fight along the Bonito banks. And Clay recalled that Robey had not even returned to bury her.

Clay knew that Robey was out to get him now. He recognized his hand of ruination in everything that was going on around him. No ranch but his own in all that valley was left unvisited or unmolested. And Clay did not wonder that the people thereabouts regarded him with hate and fear. With Robey, vengeance was an art and passion.

Clay took to spending more time than ever in the saddle. With Clint and Efigio he would devote endless hours to patrolling his land. His one hope lay in finding some one of that bunch on the prowl. He knew his only chance of vindication lay in bringing one of the Moore bunch in. But after Diamond-Back's visit they left him scrupulously alone, and Clay could not hunt them on another man's range. The pine-tree brand was not welcome on neighboring land.

He knew that something was bound to break, and soon. Robey was sinking his teeth on the average of once a week and bands of armed men were searching through the countryside. There could have been an element of humor in that because Clay knew that Robey could not be caught that way; but there was a chilling quality in it, for he did not know but what those same bands might wreak their wrath on him. Guns in concert were inclined toward restlessness.

He disliked the thought of going into town at all, but there were times when he could not avoid it. A good many things that they required could be found nowhere else. It had one time been Efigio's duty and pleasure to make that frequent trek, but Clay would not assign it to him anymore. The element of danger was too great these days, and he did not want to expose the Mexican to an unprovoked attack.

But he had to go himself, and while it was not the enjoyable thing that it had been many years ago he never ceased to wonder at the changes time had wrought. That town down there was growing up. It had one time been a kind of cattle crossing at the junction of the Pecos and the Hondo, but now the old-timers wouldn't recognize it. Among other things the people down there were putting the rivers to work. A body was one time content to sit up there on the high ground when the day's work was done and watch those rivers carry on their never-ending dreams. But now they were digging ditches and plowing the lowlands and electing one another mayor-domos of the new acequias. There was a whole new crowd down there now, a storekeeping crowd, that would sell you anything you could think of. They had called it Roswell, now, for half a decade.

Clay had to go down there one day and he was very conscious of the alterations. They somehow made him feel like more of an outsider than he really was. It was nothing like the old times when he would go down that way with Hardin in the spring wagon. A body could look for miles in that by-gone day and see little more than nothing, but now his eyes were filled with man's creations in any direction he might choose to look: men plowin', men layin' shiny barbed wire, men buildin' cabins and homes along the watercourses. A far cry from the time when John Chisum's ranch house was about the only civilized mark in all that vastness, if you wasn't to count those adobe heaps that Van Smith had built at first. Folks even said Pat Garret was tinkering with the notion of trying to bring in artesian wells. It was enough to make any memory-minded man shake his head.

Clay rode down there that day with his gun on his hip. He didn't have his nose set for trouble, but a body never knew. It sometimes seemed that those that wanted peace the most were those who got the least of it. And he wasn't taking any chances.

It was hot in those streets, and crowded. It was late summer, going into autumn, and the warm air hung thick with dust. There were more contrivances in that street than he'd ever seen before at any one time, except for those he'd seen in Santa Fe; rigs, traps, big, steel-rimmed wagons and simple wooden-wheeled carretas, all kicking up their share of dirt. And the people that went with them. Gawdalmighty.

There was nearly every sort of person he had ever heard of, and they were all in a hurry. All going somewhere, or coming from some place else. A lot of them were country-folk, Mexicans, cattlemen and ranchers and the like, but a good many more weren't, or anyhow, didn't appear to be.

The clothes those people wore had surely never come from that town. They were brought-on things, from the far east, likely. Maybe as far away as Kansas City or St. Louis, or, by Judas, Chicago even. Fellers walkin' along, or ridin' on a horse or in a light trap, wearing slick grey pants and a checkered vest and a gold chain across the middle of 'em; with shiny boots, knee-high, and all topped off with a big hat near as high as the smokestack of that Santa Fe train he'd ridden on. Only thing missing was the sparks and smoke.

And the women-folk, glory be to God. Prancing along the boardwalks and underneath the building galleries just like fillies. Women-folk wearing little bits of high-laced black shoes and flimsy print dresses, thin and swishy, maybe giving a hint of what was underneath. With bonnets on their heads, tied beneath the chin with a ribbon of some kind and maybe a scoop-like brim coming out over their faces, that made a body want to peek around inside. Well, some of them, anyway. And parasols, shading out the sun, and like to poke your eye out if you got too close or didn't watch where you were going. He wondered how his Ma would take to all this; his Ma and her linsey-woolsey and her flat-heeled clumsy shoes. That was back a time, all right.

He did what he had come to do, and then he hung around a bit. It probably wasn't good sense, but a body didn't get to see things like this very often, unless he lived here, something Clay didn't hanker for. It was all right to have a town like this handy and nearby to come to when a person took a notion, but he surely wouldn't want to make it permanent. Too many people to crowd him, too much noise getting in amongst his thinking, too much slops and garbage spilling out of upstairs windows, not enough room to move around in. Breathing another man's breath when he was done with it.

Clay tied the Morgan to the hitch-rail before a place called the Big Chance and mixed with the crowd keeping small and inconspicuous. He kept his mouth shut and his eyes open and he saw a lot of people that he knew. Rocking on the front veranda of the new-built hotel, Old Man Medford was passing the time of the day with a pair of levi-wearing range-riders. In an upstairs window, not far down the street, he got a glimpse of Dodge Liston palavering with someone in an office he kept there in town. Even at that distance Dodge looked clean and calm, as though the heat and dust showed a special consideration where he was concerned. Through a swinging batwing he saw Steve Gallagher dealing in a poker game. Jack Harris sat beside him, waiting for his hole card.

Clay kept on walking. He went slowly down the street, turned and crossed it and came back up on the other side. He walked below the gallery roof shielding Dodge from the eyes of those directly underneath him, wondering what kind of sly maneuvering Dodge was engaging in above. He sauntered past the hotel veranda and sensed rather than saw Old Man Medford bring his rocker down and take his feet from the rail as he went on past. He kept on going and didn't look back. Let the old coot wonder.

There were crowds and streams of people all around, and he was into the one that had the trouble for him before he knew it or could do anything to change it. A handful of men, maybe half a dozen or so, were lazing and talking on the wide front stoop of mercantile store. Some sitting, some standing, some talking in the group, some simply gazing around. When Clay went threading through them a big man with a coarse, wide face with a voice to match said, "Hanged if it ain't Clay Forest. You bring Robey into town with you?"

Clay turned sharp; he maybe should have run right then, but he didn't. He turned and looked this big man over. He was one of those who sometimes feel it incumbent upon them to have words with any handy man of reputation or notoriety; one of those who run up a gunman's score. Clay saw this all at once, and he saw that he was half-way drunk as well;

halfway drunk and stupid in the eyes and loud and big-talking because of it. Grinning, now, like he maybe attached a special importance to himself because he'd spoken out.

Clay looked him over close. He was mad inside. He saw this big-mouthed man and he knew he was a trouble-hunter. He wore a frontier leather jacket with fringe on the sleeves and his hair was cut long and dirty to his shoulders. He had an odor like a stable.

"Any argument to me walkin' through here?" Clay said to him.

The coarse-faced man hooked his thumbs in a wide gun-belt.

"Some might have, given they knew who you was."

"You one of 'em?" Clay said.

They were three, maybe four, feet apart, facing one another in the center of the stoop. The others were becoming more attentive now. Clay could feel them easing off and making room the way that men did when there was shooting imminent and they were being careful of it. He knew the big man was the gunhand in the crowd. The others wouldn't have the stomach for a part in it, 'less it was maybe side-winding from a safe place and distance. He wasn't afraid of anything from them.

The big man let his eyes drift around before he said anything again. "I could be one of 'em," he said then. "We like a clean town here. I could be one o' 'em, all right, Forest."

Clay let his shoulders loosen up. Clay thoughts were running through his head. Was his Colt hammer sitting on an empty, or on a live round? What about this man, was this a trap of some kind? Was there another maybe drawing a bead on his back from an upstairs window across the street?

"You better make up your mind," he said. "I ain' got all day."

It happened fast. For all his size and seeming muddle-headedness, the big man moved quick. It was silent with the tight quiet of waiting, and then it all broke open and the high-faced board buildings threw the guns' roaring back at them. Clay felt the wide blast of hot concussion smash with a soft blow all over him and he saw the big man step back and then turn and walk crazy-drunk-like a few steps and then fall over. He felt the new shock get into everyone and those around made a wide alley as he went through and commenced to run across the street. He got to the Morgan and swung on up. He'd like to hurry but he knew he couldn't; too many horses, too many people, too many rigs and wagons. He walked the Morgan toward the nearest side street. Looking back once, he saw the crowd closing in around the fallen dead man. A curl of smoke rose up from the middle of them, and as they parted he saw the dead man's clothing burning.

He put the Morgan at a dead run for the ranch. He'd started something now, all right. Things had maybe been sitting in a kind of doubtful balance, but they weren't that way anymore. Those around who were waiting for a sure-fire provocation had one now. It didn't make any difference that the other'd been the one to start the business, to make a move to draw first; that was all done now, and they had what they were looking for. Blame them, anyway, a body just couldn't have no peace. Couldn't live his life as he saw fit to. They'd be coming now, soon maybe, as quick as they got organized; and everything was changed again. Damn that drunken lout.

Efigio and Lupe were waiting for him in the dooryard, looking like they'd maybe had a premonition, the way that people of that blood sometimes did. People of the land and soil those near to God and nature, sometimes seemed to get a message far-off like.

"We see you coming fast, Clay," Efigio said. "Sí, yes, we see you coming and there is trouble now, no?"

"All kinds of it, I reckon," Clay said. "Had a scrap in town, killed a feller—big gun-tough they had hangin' around there." It all came out in scenes and pieces as he dismounted and looked around them in the dooryard. It seemed that he was far away and that none of it was real. But he knew it was.

Efigio made a low whistle, his mustachios dipping at the corners of his mouth. "Ho, we fight, then, I think. Soon they come and we fight."

"No, we ain't goin' to fight no one," Clay said. "Wouldn't have a chance against 'em all. We got to get out for awhile, till this thing simmers down. We got to find another way."

Lupe flapped her apron at a buzzing fly. "Get out? Leave this place? I have dinner cooking. How can we go now?"

"Well, we got to; we ain't got much time. We'll have to take what we can use and leave the rest, and hope they don't burn the place when they get here. Where's Clint?"

Efigio turned around and scowled toward the slow rise lifting behind the buildings. "He is up there someplace. A while ago he think he maybe see Diamond-Back up there and we go together, but there is nothing. When I come back he thinks he look a little more."

"Oh, God," Clay said. "As if one thing ain't enough. Well, I better go get him, then. You get your things together and start moving. I'll get back here as quick as I can, but don't wait. Take only what you need, we've got to travel light. Better head off toward Hondo, get into the hills and timber. You got kin-folk up there, ain't you, Efigio?"

"Sí, we go there, Clay; but, first, I come with you to get Clint."

"No," Clay said. "You got to stay here and get Lupe out; there ain't the time."

Lupe was staring into the darkness beyond the door of the house. "But, Clay, there is the dinner; in just a little while."

Clay took hold of Lupe's shoulder gently. "No time, Lupe; we got to go. Bring some of it if you can, but we can't stay here and eat it."

Efigio sighed as he got used to the new idea, but Lupe stood rigidly, not willing to accept it yet. "So, well, we get ready," Efigio said. "We wait a little bit for you here, Clay. We take what we can from here."

Lupe's eyes became suddenly liquid as she began to understand it and to realize the inevitability. "Sí, we go," she said, and she went inside and left them there.

Clay waited for Efigio to run off toward the barn before he put the Morgan around the corral and toward the rise to the north. As he went up higher he could look back and see everything dozing quietly in the sun. It seemed like nothing bad or unsettling could ever happen in that place and yet it was. A man could never know what could overtake him from one moment in his life to the next. It made him sour and bitter and he swore at everything.

A little ways up he passed the place where he had seen Clint that day and a bit beyond that, the one where Diamond-Back had laid with his rifle in the grass; Clint had shown him that. Still further, he rode parallel with the arroyo where he had stalked Dodge Liston in the heat and dust. Remembering those things now, it seemed that a great stretch of time had intervened between those incidents and this, but he knew it hadn't. It was just a few weeks, a month or more, and everything was ended.

Near the north end of the arroyo he saw Clint's horse. He didn't see it right away because it was grazing over behind a growth of yucca and he was nearly upon it before he realized its presence. He dismounted and approached the animal with caution though he did not know exactly why. He was thinking that it was a good horse and that Clint had always taken care of it. He was thinking that this affection had been returned by the horse and that it rarely left the vicinity where Clint might be. He had a sick apprehension inside him because of knowing this.

The horse looked up and made a small whinny and went on grazing. Clay took hold of the bridle and ran his hands along the neck and belly, as though looking for some kind of clue or other. Coming around in back of it, he was on the lip of the arroyo and he looked down. The sun's glare was white and hot in the alkali and the baked earth threw the reflection into his face and eyes. It made Clint's body look mirage-like, suspended in the waves of heat. It made it look like it was still vibrating with life and being, but he knew it wasn't. The hot sun had already caused the blood to crust about the wide hole between Clint's shoulders. He did not have to go down in there to know Clint Rhodes was dead.

· CHAPTER 8 ·
Talk With Your Gun

HE GOT AWAY FROM THE RANCH SOMEWHAT LATER THAN he thought he would, but there was still time. There had been a lot to do. After he buried Clint out there he came back and he was glad that Efigio and Lupe had already gone. What time was left he wanted for himself.

He felt like a ghost walking through those lonesome rooms. He kept remembering those early days and while they had been hard, what with building the place and making it pay, they had been happy and satisfying ones as well. Until the Lincoln fight there had been a kind of peace and happiness about it all. Hardin and his Ma had known they were building for the future. They had worked hard and long, but that never seemed to bother them. His Ma had always said that the length of a person's life never mattered, it was what that person did with the time he had. She had lived that way and died that way, and so had Hardin. And they had built this place and left it in his care.

It made him wonder if he was doing the right thing in going off again and leaving it as he was. It made him think that he maybe ought to hole up here with his guns and ammunition and what food Lupe and Efigio had not taken, and let them come and drag him out. It would likely be a noble thing to do.

But he had a strong notion that Hardin and his Ma would not approve of that. A thing like that was too rooted in primitive instinct and a wise man would go off somewhere and watch and listen and wait for his turn. A wise man knew when the odds were too great to be worthy of consideration. He never got anywhere by being impetuous and losing his head in some vainglorious action.

He took his leave of the place some two or three hours ahead of sunset. He left everything in the house pretty much as it had been and took the Morgan and the other horses in the string down the cottonwood alley, and swung off to the west. Half a mile beyond the buildings, he turned the remuda loose and watched the horses wander off, some of them now and then lifting or turning their heads to look at him. In their own way they likely wondered, too.

After that he took his time and waited. He kept the Morgan going along the faint trail slowly, tracing the general direction which he knew that Lupe and Efigio had taken. Perhaps he should have hurried but he had to see the end of it. He had to see what was going to happen at the ranch.

He was fairly high above it when the long spine of dust came winding up the valley from Roswell far below. He could only see the long, snaking funnel of it in the beginning, not giving much thought to the number of riders that might be making it. But it came onward in a hurry, and kept clinging to the trail to the Pine-Tree range. When it turned into the cottonwood lane he felt the apprehension gnawing at him once again. The men in that posse were angry men and there was likely no accounting for their actions. He kept thinking that they might shoot the place up, smash the furnishings, and even burn it to the ground. He kept hoping there were sober minds as well.

It seemed damned peculiar sitting up there like that, watching those men ride into his dooryard, stomping on his gallery and pushing through the doors into his house, like they owned the place, and him not daring to show his nose down there or lift a finger to prevent whatever it might be that they were going to do. Just seeing them do that drove a goad into him, made a voice shout at him inside to go on down there again and drive them out, or perish in the trying.

Dusk was coming on when he saw the first light shining soft through a window of the house, and an involuntary sigh went out of him. He knew it was all right now. They were not going to fire it, at least. There would likely be some of them staying on a while to see if he was coming back or not, but the place would stand. He was sure of that.

When some of the group mounted up again and went like shadows down the alley and back toward town he got back on the Morgan and headed west once more. It was coming on night and the far-off mountains looked like humped cripples crouching in the dying light. Somewhere in those mountains Robey Moore was likely waiting. Thinking of that gave rise to a cold-hot sensation inside him somewhere. In his own way, Robey had been right all along, he was thinking. Robey'd one time said he'd get him back. And, by God, Robey was going to get him; only maybe in a way he hadn't thought of. One of them would never leave those mountains. There was no other way anymore. No other way at all.

* * *

He kept along the Hondo, heading toward the Capitans. He had never thought he'd be going into those hills for a purpose such as this one, but he was doing it. His destiny seemed as rooted in their soil as the pine and fir and cedar bursting from their heights. Nearly every guiding force of his young life had had its generation in those mountains. A special kind of fate seemed to lurk for him up there. A malevolent kind of magnet seemed to draw him toward those green broad bosoms.

His mind kept turning back to the last time he'd come up to those mountains from the valley down below. He kept remembering how he'd gone back home after the fight at Blazer's Mill, and how he'd tried to take up ranching once again. He kept remembering how he'd been busted up with Robey, and how he'd felt lost and at loose ends because he knew the Lincoln scrap hadn't wholly ended just because he'd gotten out of it. He remembered how he'd one day gone back, and what had happened all because of it.

The day he got to Lincoln was a fine one, he remembered that. It was bright and clear and sharp-smelling, the way that only a mountain town can be. Lincoln lay against a steep uprising of the mountain wall and the old adobe and timber buildings stood out sharp and well-defined against the rock and timber rising up; Murphy's place, the bank, the McSween-Tunstall store.

But if the day was good the time was not. The people in that town were as sore and angry as a hive of displaced hornets. Since he had felt compelled to return to that country, he could have picked a better time. He had got there only shortly after the last big battle of the year. It had happened in that very town and local spirit and temper were shaken to their roots. McSween and Murphy, ringleaders and organ-

zers, were dead and buried, but the town was seeth-
ing still. The hired killers had departed for the most
part and the brutalized villagers were in the market
for a scapegoat for the violations of those men. Clay
could have picked a better time, all right.

He tied the Morgan to the hitch before the hotel
and walked down the street. The McSween store was
still smoking softly in the blue air and that made
him get a creepy feeling up his back. He knew something big had happened. On the hotel gallery, an old
man told him what had come to pass. This old man
did not recognize him and he gave freely of what
he'd seen and heard.

"Yessir, sonny, if'n it's fightin' a body likes then
that body should have been here four days back.
There was surely enough to suit most anyone."

Clay had this uneasy feeling in him and he was
careful to keep his face beneath the shadow of his
hat. Already, he was beginning to curse himself for
coming up here. Why in hell hadn't he stayed down
at the ranch? He had his belly full, why hadn't he
stayed where he belonged?

"I seen that buildin' smokin' over there; was there
fightin' in it?"

"There surely was, right in there and all around
it." The old guy slide a sidewise glance at Clay. "That
there place is the McSween-Tunstall store; ain't you
been here before? You somehow seem familiar."

Clay lied as gracefully as he could. "No," he said.
"I ain't never been up here before. Just more or less
goin' through. To Carrizozo. Yeah, that's where I'm
goin'."

The old man took a bite of plug and some of the
juice flowed mustard-yellow in his whiskers. "Well,
that's where it was all right. McSween holed up in
here with Charlie Bowdre and O'Folliard and Billy
Bonney—they're takin' to callin' him the Kid now, a
devil in human form—and a bunch of others and they

all fought it out with Murphy's outfit. Even the Fort Stanton troopers was in it for a spell."

"The hell you say," Clay said. He tried to think it out; it must have been a battle royal.

"Yup. Feller named Chavez brung some greasers up to side McSween, and Colonel Dudley got him some Gatlings down here and said did one greaser pull a trigger the Neds would go into action. They took the hint and cleared out. After that it was only time."

"Was it the troopers burned the place?" Clay asked.

"Nope, they just kind of stood around and watched. Murphy's bunch took care of the fire; I mean the bunch that worked for him—him bein' dead from sickness just a bit. But they set her afire and when she got goin' good them inside made a break. I was in a upstairs winder and I seen everythin'. They come pourin' out 'o there like rats, and there was so much shootin' it sounded like an avalanche."

"Well, I'll be blamed," Clay said. "Who was in it? I mean who was hit?"

"A lot of 'em was hit. Yessir, a whole lot. McSween was the first. They was waitin' for him in particular and he went down weighin' maybe twenty pounds more'n normal. Harvey Morris went down, too, and a couple of Mexicans. On Murphy's side, Bob Beckwith got it from Billy the Kid, and the rest of the Kid's bunch got away. It was gettin' on to dark then, and they made it all right."

By God, Clay thought. Murphy dead, McSween dead—the Lincoln war was over. Weren't no gunhands going to stay around 'less they was paid, and there was no one now to pay 'em. By God, he could go on back home for certain now. He could go on back home and never leave again.

He tried to keep it out of his voice and manner. He asked another question.

"I didn't hear you mention Robey Moore. I don't suppose his gang was in on it."

The old man was quiet for a moment and Clay felt a tight thing get into his throat and neck. The old man's eyes were sliding around toward him again, with a far-off remembrance creeping into them. His voice got careful.

"Moore? No, don't recall his gang was here, though they're known to be around here now. Folks figure they're runnin' beef."

The old guy was looking squarely at Clay now, his mouth dipped slightly open so Clay could see the plug inside it. "What'd you say your name was, sonny?"

"I don't guess I did," Clay said. Clay pulled at his hat. He hitched at his trousers and commenced to head for the steps of the veranda. Gawdalmighty, what a fool he'd been! Bringin' up Robey's name like that. Gettin' that old gossip's mind along a different track. He could feel the old guy's eyes boring into his back, suspicious, maybe dead certain. It made him walk fast, stiff. Then the voice sliced between his shoulders, shrill, filling the street with sound.

"Hey! I know you! You rode with Moore! Gol-dang it, you're that Forest feller!"

Clay kept on going. He wanted to break and run, but he couldn't. All them people looking at him now. Where the devil had they come from? They hadn't been out there before, hadn't seemed so, anyway. He had to get away from them. He had to get around a corner somehow; out of sight. Then work back to the Morgan, and get out of town. God, what a fool he'd been!

A pair of young girls stared at him in awe, then screamed. An old Mexican woman with a basket on her head commenced to run in front of him, flapping across the ground like a chicken of some kind. The basket toppled and streamed laundry in the road. All around him folks were yelling now and pointing at him, running.

He got around the corner of the hotel and slunk down the side of it and to the rear. The cry was a regular chant behind him. He could hear it everywhere. They had the scent and they had to have the kill. He kept on going.

He came around the rear and worked toward the other side of it. There was a lot of noise behind him and he knew he had to hurry. The edge of panic was cutting into his nerves and he got careless once again. He turned the far corner and nearly ran Dad Peppin down; Dad Peppin, ex-Murphy man, now sheriff. Clay saw the big star and stood there. Peppin's eyes bulged and he stood stock-still, afraid to draw.

Clay could have killed him and he knew it. He could have killed him and got out, maybe, but he didn't. He had no record of any kind in that place that could be held against him. He'd been no hired gunslick; he'd fought the Lincoln war with his conscience. All this sang through his head in those few seconds.

Dad Peppin licked his lips. "Well, now, Forest, what you goin' to do?"

Clay kept his hands low, shoulders hunched ahead. "Depends on what you want me for. I didn't come up here for trouble."

"Maybe. Maybe not. The people in this place ain't sure, though. They've had enough of killin'. They want to know."

"You want to talk about it?"

"Might be best. You want to come with me?"

Clay thought it over, listening to the chase coming around the far side of the building. It wouldn't be

ong now and there'd be real trouble. He'd have to
do his talking with his gun, then.

"All right," he said. "I'll go with you."

So he went. Dad Peppin took him to the old Murphy store, which was being used for those things now
that Murphy was dead. They locked him up in there
and three days later they filed a charge against him.

For the murder of a man he'd never seen. With a
name he'd never heard before.

Coming into the hills again after two years and
more brought that all back into his head and made
it fresh and green. He'd always been good about remembering details—Hardin had taught him that in
the hills and forests—and he could remember everything there was to know about the day they got him
and the days after that in the Murphy store at Lincoln; the trial, the hostile people jamming into that
place, the judge batting away at flies all the time and
hardly listening to what was being said, the testimony of a missing and unknown witness pinning the
killing on him—testimony that was allowed whether
the witness was there to take a Bible oath or not.

But that was enough. That's all they had to have.
That's all they wanted. They had him there and there
was nothing else to it. Two years, they said to him.
Make it more if he'd been actually seen to pull the
trigger. But he was seen standing near the dead man,
and that was good enough for two.

Well, that's the way it was, and coming on up to
these knowing old hills brought it all out for him to
look at once again. Brought it all out and he could
wonder how it happened, and know that, if it hadn't
been for the Lincoln war he never would have gone
to jail for anything. But thinking about those things
now didn't have any bearing on the present. They
didn't have much to do with what he was getting set
for now. Stirring up his feelings with those old mem-

ories wasn't going to keep him cool and calm for Robey Moore.

On the second evening he went around Hondo and got into the real hill and forest country. Efigio had said his kin-folks were up this way and he thought it likely that he and Lupe had stopped up there to wait and see. Several miles along the Lincoln road he saw a cluster of adobe huts off to the side some that seemed to answer the description that Efigio had given him one time. He got down from his horse and led him over that way.

It was a warm and quiet night and the sounds from those casas carried far. He didn't like to go poking around in another person's property after dark and he strained his ears to hear a voice that could be Lupe's or Efigio's. He got in real close against a wall but he heard nothing that he seemed to recognize.

Then he turned around and saw a figure in the starlight. It was standing there behind him, and must have been there all along. He got scared and angry all at once, and then he heard the gentle laughter.

"Clay?" the voice said.

"Yeah," Clay said. "It's me, Efigio."

"I wait for you here in the bushes. Sapristi, you are long in coming! I wait forever, I think."

"Yeah, I know. I had to bury Clint."

They were standing fifteen feet apart in the star light, looking at one another. There was a crazy qual ity about it, as though each was from a different world.

"Clint? Bury him?"

"Yeah. I found him up there. Up there where he'd gone. I guess Diamond-Back was up there after all Clint didn't have a chance."

• CHAPTER 9 •
Outlaws All the Way

CLAY ROLLED UP IN A BLANKET AND SPENT THE NIGHT IN the open. He did not like to sleep inside when he was away from the ranch. In strange places, he found it better to have room around him. It was no good to be closed in where he would have no place to go if he was called upon to move. The time spent previously in these hills had conditioned him to that, and he was used to it.

Besides, there was too much noise inside. Efigio's kinfolk were numerous and of all descriptions. There were infants, and they cried and fussed incessantly; and there were mothers or aunts or grown sisters who ministered to them and made more noise in doing so. And the men were drinking tequila and mescal and talking politics endlessly. The more they drank the more they talked and the louder and more vociferous they became. One of them, an old uncle who was called Hernandez Pasquale, was agitating for a revolution. He was one who had learned to do

fine silver-work from a Navajo, but that did not mak
any difference when he was drinking and talking po
itics in the evening. It made Clay think about th
unhappiness of people like him. They always wante
something different, and when they had it the
wanted something different still. It made him thin
that such happiness as they had was derived fro
the strife and turmoil of their unhappiness. It wa
not a clear thought, and he went to sleep while tr
ing to unravel it.

He explained everything to Efigio in the mornir
as he was getting ready to ride. He explained abou
the killing of Clint and of his determination to brir
an end to Robey Moore because of it. He told hir
there was no other way because Moore would nev
stop until he had been made to do so forcibly.

"Then it is very simple," Efigio said when Clay wa
done with it. "We will go and find him and do wha
must be done, and then go home again."

Clay did not like the idea of Efigio getting into
and he said so. "I'd better do this alone. These ar
bad men and they stop at nothin'."

"So? Then two of us will be better," Efigio said.

"No. You don't know this kind. They're bad all th
way through them."

"Well, I have known men of that sort before. I ar
not afraid."

"I didn't say you were. I just said they're ba
Backshooters and everythin'. Outlaws all the wa
They kill for the fun of it."

"Then I must surely come with you. You canno
do it alone."

Clay finished with the horse and looked aroun
The sun was coming through the trees and those i
the casa were making waking noises and squintir
through the door and paneless windows. Inside, h
could hear someone grinding corn between a pair c
metates, and he thought that would be Lupe. H

wondered if Hernandez Pasquale was still snoring on his pallet or arguing politics some more.

"What about Lupe?" he said. "You can't go runnin' off and leavin' her. Supposin' you get shot. Then what?"

Efigio shrugged. "It will be all right. Anyway, she will be happy here while we are gone. All of these mouths to cook for. Yes, she will be in paradise."

What the hell, Clay thought, what the hell. "All right," he said. "Don't blame me when you're spittin' blood, remember that."

"Sí, yes, I remember that. If I die I tell the Diós that you warned me; I tell Him everything. He will be good to you for that."

Efigio went around to the rear of the casa to get his horse and Clay swung up on the Morgan and waited for him. Efigio's kin-folk were coming out of the casa, now, and regarding him with big and solemn eyes. It occurred to him that they had known all along what he had come there for. He had not told them, and Efigio had not known until just now, but still they had known. These people were like that, he thought. They had a sense for death and trouble. They had a nose for death stalking round about.

When Efigio came back on his horse he removed his hat and bowed to all of them. "Adios," he said. "We see you soon."

They stood there watching them. The old uncle came through the door and bowed in return. The early sun made the grey in his hair shine like the fine filigrees of silver which he worked, and he inclined his head with great dignity. He did not look like a revolutionary now.

"May success attend you, and may the good Diós ride at your side."

"Gracias," Efigio said.

The others said nothing and Clay's eyes strayed to Lupe. She was standing a little apart and he wondered how a person so round and utterly shapeless could in one particular moment appear as straight and magnificent as she was now. There was the strength and ageless knowledge of the mountains in her face.

"And may the Madre guard and keep you," she said.

And that was all. They rode away from the casa toward the trail. It was very quiet all around them and each hoof made a clear, distinct sound as it was placed upon the ground.

They rode west by north and the day was beautiful. They kept the Hondo on their left and made the beginning of an arc to take them around Lincoln without going through it. Clay had nothing to fear in that town anymore, but he did not want to be seen in that vicinity. There was always the chance of a stray word getting on to Robey, and he knew they would need all the secrecy they could get. So they stayed off the main roads and kept to those trails little used.

For the most part they went ahead in silence. Clay was thinking about a great many diverse things and he knew that Efigio must be doing likewise. A man did not go out easily to court his own destruction; he always had some thoughts about it. It did not make much difference what kind of person he had been before that moment. There came a time when he had to sort these things out privately. He had to get into a certain frame of mind.

After a time he told Efigio where they were heading for. He felt positive that Robey and the bunch would have headed for the high ground after the killing of Clint and the latest depredations in the valley, and he knew that Efigio ought to know about his reasoning on that.

"Every time they do something like that they lay low," he said. "They always get off in the timber and sit around. I figure that's what they're doin' now. Like as not they know they got me into as big a jam as I can be got into, and they're goin' to see what happens next."

"You think they know about that one in town? The one with whom you fight?"

"I don't know. Maybe. Wouldn't surprise me none. Robey always seemed to know just what he ought to know. What'd do him good to know."

"You think, then, they are up here?" Efigio said. "Más allá?"

"Yeah, I think so. I figure if we can find Steve Howard we can find 'em all. He used to keep company with a mujer up here not far from Encinosa. Used to spend some time up there after every bit of trouble. Seems natural for him to be there now."

"Is that the one whose father had the sheep? The one you tell me about whose sheep were killed?"

"No. No, that ain't the one. That was Robey done that. This one ain't far from that place, though. Five, maybe ten, miles."

"You think he is there, then, this Howard?"

"Can't say for sure, but we'll see. As good a bet as any right now. He liked her pretty much. He was always weak for her."

Efigio laughed softly and Clay looked at him.

"Ho, that is a good one. A bad gunman who is weak for one of those. For the girls."

"Yeah, Steve's like that," Clay said. "That's why I figured we'd look him up first. If he's there he'll talk. By God, how he'll talk."

They kept going, but they took their time. Clay wanted to get to this place in the evening and so they did not hurry. It was not much more than twenty miles between the casa of Efigio's kinfolk and that of the mujer with whom Steve Howard sometimes kept company, and so there was no rush about it. It was simply a matter of timing.

They commenced to ease down from the higher country once again. Toward mid-afternoon they had worked through the backbone of the Capitans and they were once more in the foothills. There was piñon and aspen and great pine all about them and along the trail they traveled. Clay liked the aspen especially, and kept remembering how the leaves had always trembled and quivered in golden grandeur in the fall; their slim trunks like ivory columns.

It was nightfall when Clay saw the small light ahead of them, and he knew they had arrived. The place in which they were was familiar to him now, and he knew the light was one of those from the casa of Howard's mujer. How many times he had ridden through here before he could not readily recall, but he had done it frequently with Robey. Robey always had to come and get Steve away from her when it was time for them to go again.

They left their horses in the timber and covered the remaining distance on foot. They circled the building once to get the lay of the land, and counted the horses in the small pole corral at the rear. There were two in there. Two horses and a burro. All of them were dozing and did not pay them any heed.

At the front of the casa they stooped down behind a low and thorny thrust of brush. Inside, they could hear voices and Clay did not think anything was suspected. There was simply a conversational drone, punctuated by laughter and snatches of garbled singing.

"Shall we go right in?" Efigio said to him.

"Maybe we better," Clay said. "Surprise 'em is the best way."

"Yes. Perhaps. But that would not be polite."

Clay looked at Efigio and saw that he was smiling. Efigio's long mustachios had a humorous twist to them, which pleased him, because he knew that Efigio felt good about it. Efigio was the right one to have with him for a thing like this.

They crept toward the door. "You maybe better hang back here and watch them windows," Clay said before they come to it. "No sense in bein' foolish about it."

"No. All right. I do that. I watch the windows." Efigio paused and pulled his gun from its holster. Clay had never paid it much attention before, but he saw now that it was an old Colt with a short, ugly barrel. Efigio smiled when he noticed Clay's glance. "It is a good one," he said. "It has a fine spring. It is just right."

Clay nodded and went up on the low stoop. It was quiet inside now, a waiting quiet, and Clay had the fear that they had made too much noise. Directly against the inner panel of the door, he heard a body moving, then a voice.

"Quién es?" it said. "Quién es?"

Clay did not answer. He crouched there, tight inside, his gun clamped in his fingers. His breathing sounded like a high wind.

"Damn it all," another voice said, "sit down." And Clay recognized Ed Picket's.

"I heard somethin', I tell you," the first one said again, and because it was distinct this time Clay knew it was Howard's. "I heard talkin' out there."

"Perhaps it was the horses." A girl's voice, with light banter in it. "The burro, he is always talking; perhaps he was making conversation with your horses. He is very courteous."

Clay heard Steve Howard make a rude sound with his lips. Then the door opened and a thin slice of light cut across the stoop. Clay pressed against the dried mud and waited. When it opened further and Howard poked his head out Clay swung the gun around and pushed it into Howard's belly.

"Hello, Steve," he said.

Howard stood there. His face looked loose, like an old shirt. His lips were moving but no sound was coming out of them. Clay reached out with his other hand and got hold of Howard's belt. He jerked him through the door and out of the light. At the same time, Ed Picket swore and smashed the light out; the girl screamed, then whimpered as something struck her. Picket's fist, likely, Clay thought. Ed always was short on patience.

Clay kept hold of Howard's belt until he got him out of line with the door and the one window on that side of the house. He knew that Howard was still astonished, but that it was wearing off. He was wary enough to leave his gun alone, though.

"Damn you, Forest, what you think you're doin'?" he said.

"I come for a talk with you," Clay said. "I come to find where Robey is."

"You did, huh. Well, I don't know."

Clay swung the gun in a fast arc and raked Howard's face with the front sight. Steve Howard stumbled backwards and Clay raked the other side of it. He remembered the way he'd pistol-whipped the man who killed his father, but he felt different about this. He felt glad inside. Everything was coming out of him and he felt glad. He kept smashing at Howard's face until the other man sank to his knees. Howard groped blindly, sobbing, for Clay's legs, more in supplication than in offense. His voice was hollow and filled with bubbles.

"Forest," he said. "Forest, Gawdalmighty, Forest."

Clay hit him once more, then stopped. "Where is he, Steve? Tell me where he is."

Howard tried for Clay's legs again and Clay stepped back.

"He'll kill me if I tell; God, Forest, you know how

he is. You know how Robey is. He'll kill me, I tell you. Just last week he killed Bob Fergus for no reason at all—for no reason at all."

"No, he won't," Clay said. "Robey'll never get near you."

Howard was on his hands and knees, his head down. Even in the starlight Clay could see the blood stream darkly, dripping on the ground.

"He's up on the Ruidoso," Steve Howard said weakly. "He's up there with Diamond-Back. They're stayin' up near Bowdre's old place. Up near where your pa was killed that time."

Clay put his gun in the holster and rested his hands on his hips.

"All right, Steve. You can get up now."

Steve Howard raised his head and looked at Clay.

"What you goin' to do?"

"Get up," Clay said. "I'm givin' you an even break. More'n you ever gave to anyone. More'n my man, Clint Rhodes, got."

"Wait a minute. Listen, Forest, listen, you got me all wrong. Listen, damn it, Robey's your man, not me. For God's sake, Forest, listen! Robey done everything to you! He even got you framed at Lincoln!"

Clay felt the hair at his neckline lift. "What?"

"God, yes! Nobody can get away from him. He swore he'd fix you when you put your gun on him at Blazer's Mill. That Lincoln thing was just a starter. He was set to keep on you as long as you lived. He's the one gave Peppin and them the notion that you could have done that killin'. He knew the notion was all they needed. That town was hot, then. They was fed up with everythin'."

"That was it, huh," Clay said. "All right, Steve, thanks."

"Forest! Listen!"

Clay stood there. It happened as he knew it would. Howard got to his knees, then dropped and rolled.

At the same time his shoulder jerked and his gun whipped up from his leg. Clay heard the two guns fire at the same time and watched Steve Howard sink down and sprawl flat. He hadn't been aware of firing, but he was holding his gun and there was Howard; lying there, grotesque and shapeless.

Clay turned around and walked back toward the casa. When he came around the corner he heard one more solitary shot, and that was all. Efigio was standing at the corner and Ed Picket was lying halfway through the window, one arm dangling toward the ground, his thick, long hair streaming across his face.

"He was curious," Efigio said. "It was only time. I simply wait. My spring, she work fine."

Inside, Steve Howard's mujer whimpered in soft spasms.

• CHAPTER 10 •
That Devil

THEY WENT BACK THROUGH THE TIMBER OF THE CAPITANS and toward the Ruidoso over south. Clay had the feel of it in him now and he was impatient to get on with it. But he knew they had to stop for food and rest. He couldn't be a fool about it. He had to use his head.

After midnight they staked out near a quiet-moving steam to the west of Lincoln. They were maybe ten miles or so to the east of Fort Stanton, and before he fell asleep Clay remembered what the old gossip in Lincoln had told him that time about Dudley bringing the troopers down. With Gatling guns and everything. That must have been a thing to see. It was still in his mind when he dropped off.

It was dawn when they were up and moving out again. Efigio had warmed up the coffee and they had finished what was left of the dried corn and beef that they had brought along. Clay had not eaten much because he was impatient and because he had this tight thing in his middle. In a way it was much the way he'd felt the day he'd ridden for the first time with Hardin, when Hardin was killed. But in another way it wasn't. He was more sure of himself, now. He knew what was going to happen and what he was going to do. He was on the giving end of it this time. But the tight thing was there just the same. It would always be whenever there was shooting to be done.

Morning in the timber was always the most beautiful time of day but Clay could not get over the sinister aspect of it. It had had that quality for him ever since the fight at Blazer's Mill. It seemed that everything dark and bad had happened or begun in the morning in those forests. The beauty of the trees was deceptive in that way. They seemed to sing of peace and rest but Clay could never forget how it had been the day they went for Buckshot Roberts.

They were full of ghosts, those woods. Much of the Lincoln fighting had been done in there, where the slow hills flowed together, then lofted up again; where the trees were tall and thick. And the ghosts of those dead and, by some, forgotten, now seemed to glide on soundless hooves among the shadows once again.

Sometimes he would steal a glance at Efigio. Sometimes he would steal a glance and wonder what was going through his mind. But Efigio's face was placid after the manner of his kind. You could never tell what men like him were thinking, it occurred to Clay. You could never tell because they always seemed to be the same, no matter what they happened to be doing.

One time Efigio noticed his covert watching, and he slapped Clay's knee and laughed.

"A fine day, yes?" he said. "A fine day for anything. How do you feel, Clay?"

"Why, I feel pretty good, I guess," Clay said. "How do you feel?"

Efigio laughed again and Clay wondered why men always talked about their state of health at a time like this. Why they were always going around asking one another how they were. Hardin had done it that day so long ago, and even Robey had not been immune to it. Robey was always trying to find out how people felt.

"Me, I feel fine, too," Efigio said. "I was just now thinking, I was just now thinking how fine I feel. I say to myself, I say, 'Efigio, you are going to have a fight in the mountains; it is a fight which has perhaps been a great while in coming and it is right that you should go. When it is done you will go back to the ranch and sit under the trees and grow old. It is a very nice place for that purpose.' "

"Yeah, that will be a great thing, all right," Clay said. "We'll get this over with and go back home and grow old."

Just saying it that way seemed to take the whole thing out of the realm of mere possibility and make it positive; he knew it was going to happen just as Efigio had said it would. They would do just as he said. They would finish with Robey. That devil.

He kept wondering why he had not been surprised at what Steve Howard had said about Robey's hand in the trial at Lincoln. It was probably because it was the most natural thing in the world for Robey to do. It was a kind of credit to him in a way. It almost made Clay admire Robey's mental agility, a thing which had always had a quality of quiet amazement for him. You never knew what to expect of Robey Moore. His approach to a problem was always different than that of someone else. It must have delighted him to have had a hand in that Lincoln business, an exquisite kind of triumph, but likely not of as great and lasting duration as he might have selected had he had the opportunity. Even so, he had had his licks; far too many. Clay thought of the Spanish father's sheep once more. That Robey, damn him to hell and all points between here and there. Damn him, damn him, damn him.

Near noon they struck the Ruidoso and turned west again. They were near now. There wasn't much distance left. Not much time left either. They couldn't be but a couple miles from Bowdre's old place. The land around there looked familiar to him. They'd ridden hell-bent through it the day that Hardin died. If he looked carefully he'd likely find the place where Pa'd gone down beneath his horse; where the Murphy man had dumped the buck-load into him. Where Robey had knocked him, Clay, silly against the big pine bole.

He had to shut those things out of his mind. He couldn't have those old incidents cluttering up his thinking, getting in the way of the business coming up. His head had to be as straight and clear as a stretch of that new Santa Fe railroad track. It had to be clean and open just like that.

When he heard the axe chucking through the trees he knew that they'd arrived. He couldn't see the cabin yet, but they got down from their horses anyway. Not many men could do their best shooting from a horse, and they couldn't take a chance on a slip of that kind. They staked them out and walked through the trees. Efigio slipped his gun out, then let it drop again. Clay made sure the button on his right shirt sleeve was fastened proper. They kept going slowly through the trees. Glory, it was quiet up in there!

Coming into the clearing, he saw Robey standing near a woodpile with the axe. Robey had his sleeves rolled up and the muscles in his lower arms bulged from the way he held the axe; he held it just slightly off the ground as he watched them coming through the trees, like he'd maybe forgotten that he had it in his hands. Not far off, a few feet maybe, Diamond-Back paused with his cupped hands raised half-way to his face, the water dripping from them into the tin basin in front of him, on a bench. Dawgonned funny to see Diamond-Back take the time and trouble to wash his face.

Clay stopped twenty yards or so away and waited. Efigio stood a couple of paces to his right, his legs slightly spread, his hat tipped back as though it might get in the way otherwise. Diamond-Back wiped his hands slowly on a dirty cloth. Robey sank the axe into the end of a butt and rolled his sleeves down. Everyone knew what was going to happen.

"Hello, Forest," Robey said. "Almost been expectin' you. Don't seem you changed much since I seen you last. Been nigh onto three years now, ain't it? Maybe two's closer. How you feel, kid?"

Clay kept watching Robey Moore. You could never tell about him. His hands were hanging natural and easy around his belt line, his right dipped back slightly, fingers partly curled. Diamond-Back was facing them directly now, his shirt wide open clear down to his navel, and the matted hair on his chest shining-like in the sun coming through the branches overhead.

"I feel pretty good, Robey," Clay said. "How do you feel?" There it was again.

Robey looked him over clinically. Robey's empty, vacant eyes drank him down and Clay commenced to feel the beginning of the strangeness he'd always had when Robey looked at him that way. Robey made a man feel more alone and solitary than anything else on earth when he put his eyes on him like that.

"Looks like you kind of leaned out," Robey said. They were sixty feet apart but it didn't make any difference. It was so still and quiet up in there that Clay could hear him perfectly.

"Yeah. Fellers do. Thanks to you I had time for it. I done most of it in jail."

Robey smiled; with his lips he smiled. "Finally figured that out, huh. Just a notion I had at the time. Hearin' they was talkin' to you down there made it too easy for me to let the chance go by."

"Steve Howard told me," Clay said. "I found him with his mujer up near Encinosa. He told me a lot before he died."

"Killed him, huh. Seems you changed quite a bit, kid. Didn't learn nothin' from that jail time, though, did yuh?"

"I learned enough. I learned there ain't nobody goin' to push me around anymore. I learned there ain't nobody goin' to make me live through hell forever."

"Sound just like your old man when you talk like that; and look what it got him."

"Ends for everybody some time, don't it?"

"Yeah, you're right about that, kid. I been kind of lookin' forward to this. I had some choppin' to do, but it can wait a bit."

Robey moved a pace or two away from Diamond-Back. "Any time, kid."

Clay's ears picked up the forest sounds around them. Without thinking about it consciously, he heard a jay-bird scatting somewhere in the pine boughs overhead. He heard a squirrel arguing further off in the blue shadows; he heard the creek washing endlessly across the rocks. The slow wind rubbing the leaves and needles against one another in a soft overtone. Nothing up here ever changed. It'd be the same when the cabin, there, was rotting in the soil. When a man's small affairs didn't amount to anything. Them same creatures, or their offspring, would be carrying on their business just the same.

He heard Efigio breathing next to him.

He kept watching Diamond-Back and Robey while these other things were coming into him. He kept watching them and waiting and he thought how Diamond-Back was the more impatient of the two. He remembered those many times when Diamond-Back had acted beyond the limits of discretion; how he didn't like to sit a thing out for very long. It was important to him that one of them should make the break. It was important that the nerves of one of them should reach the snapping point first.

It was Diamond-Back who did it. Clay saw Diamond-Back's swarthy skin stretch tight and flat across his face, and his teeth make a narrow rib of his mouth, like he couldn't keep the tension in him any longer for the thinking of it. He saw Diamond-Back make a slow hunch forward, and fork his hand down; and heard the high trees slamming the guns' roaring down upon him.

He was aware of Efigio beside him in a half crouch with his left hand fanning the hammer of the short-nosed ugly Colt and his hat all the way off now, like a bullet had maybe snatched it from his head. And he was conscious of his own firing, of the butt riding fat and heavy in his hand and of the bullets tearing big and solid into Robey, and lifting him and taking him into the woodpile and turning him again and carrying him into Diamond-Back, who was firing wildly from his knees with the muzzle of his gun aimed at everything and nothing.

And when the slug took him in the shoulder he didn't feel the pain of it, but only the soft-hard jar-ing and he kept on firing at Robey until the gun was empty and only when he tried to walk toward him did he find he couldn't move.

Then Efigio had him under the arms, and was talking to him and laughing softly into his ear. Efigio's voice was coming to him on undulating waves, now near, now very far away.

"Amigo," he was saying, "amigo, it is done, now Amigo, we have done what we have come to do. See now, how everything is finished."

And Clay stood there and leaned on Efigio and felt the strength and reality of Efigio holding him erect. He saw Diamond-Back and Robey lying smashed and twisted in the woodpile in the silence of the clearing where the cabin stood. For a great while it was the deepest silence he had ever heard. Then, way, far off the squirrel made a tentative kind of noise; and the jay-bird came down and flipped its wings in shadows across the sun-lit ground.

• CHAPTER 11 •
Trigger Trail

THE BAD SHOULDER DEVILED CLAY ALL THE WAY BACK down from the Ruidoso country to the Pecos Valley. Efigio pleaded with him to lay over a few days at his kinfolk's place, but Clay wouldn't do it. They stayed only long enough for the old uncle to plaster it with herbs, and to get Lupe in the saddle, for the homeward trek. Clay wasn't wasting any time.

Anything happening now was going to be anticlimactic, but he wanted to get it over with. There was going to be some kind of trouble down there, but he didn't give a hang about it. There wasn't much of anything that could bother him again. After Robey, he could laugh at all of them. He still had a kind of wonder in him that the whole thing was finally over, but he was getting used to it. He was going to start to live, now; the way a man out there really ought to live.

They went straight down through Roswell on the Pecos. He didn't want to take up at the ranch again until everything was squared with the people down there. He knew what they'd been thinking and he had in mind to show them he was true and honest and that their doubts on him had been all wrong. He had in mind to tell them how the end came to Robey and his bunch. That they'd never have to gun up on his account again. He'd like to do that peaceful-like if they would let him, but they could have it any way they wanted it. He hadn't forgotten Sam Chandler and the men making law down there. Nearly anything could happen. But it didn't bother him.

It had rained their last night out and the air was clean and washed above the town when they came in sight of it in the morning. There was no dust anywhere and a man could look straight on out east there until the earth curved down and there was nothing any more to see. The river had a nice glimmer to it out there and the ditches they'd been digging for the irrigating wound around out in the fields like a fine, drawn Spanish silverwork—the kind that Efigio's revolutionary uncle might do when he could put his mind to it.

When they came down and entered the street there were people all around, just like there had been before. There was more bustle in that place than a town that size really ought to have and he knew that it was growing fast. Wouldn't be long, now, before it was a regular metropolis. Likely they'd have the railroad and all that went with it one day, too, just like Dodge Liston and the others said they would. Every time he'd thought of that before this day, the town bursting up out of the ground like some strange plant, he'd had a kind of resentment smoking in him, but that was all changed now. Just so he didn't have to be in the middle of it, it would be all right. So long as he was sitting strong and prosperous out there on the ranch there was nothing any more could bother him.

About halfway down this street Clay saw Old Man Medford and the Gallaghers and Jack Harris standing beneath the hotel gallery roof, and that was all right, too. Those people were watching him in a careful kind of way and Clay had the notion that they'd seen him from a long way off. Someone had likely spotted them coming down the long slopes over west. But that was nothing for him to worry about; he didn't care. He went right up to those standing round about. He went right up to them with Efigio and they stood there looking down at them.

"Hello, Medford," Clay said. "I come back again. I got a notion you didn't expect I would. But here I am."

Old Man Medford turned a tobacco plug over in his mouth and took his time. Clay knew that none of them knew exactly what to expect of him. He knew they saw his travel stains and bloody shirt and bound up arm, and likely thought that anything could happen.

"Well, I do declare," Old Man Medford said. "You surely are back, ain't you, Clay? Can't say as we did expect you. Not after you lit out like you did that day."

"I had a lot to do and I couldn't stay around," Clay said. "I been up in the Capitans doin' your law-work for you. Me and Efigio done for Robey and his bunch."

Old Man Medford's face became a blank. "Done for Robey?"

"Killed him," Clay said. "Him and Diamond-Back and Ed Picket and Steve Howard. We'd o' killed Bob Fergus, too, only Robey done it for us. You ain't got no worry about them any more."

Steve Gallagher edged out to one side. "How do we know that's straight, Forest? We took a lot at their hands. How do we know you ain't just coverin' up or somethin'?"

"Best you go up and see for yourself," Clay said. "Howard and Picket's buried over near Encinosa— I'll tell you the place when you want to go. Robey and Diamond-Back're up at Bowdre's old place on the Ruidoso. They're under the woodpile near the cabin."

Old Man Medford's wattles were moving gently in soundless laughter. "I guess you did do for 'em, didn't you?"

"We done it, all right. Diamond-Back shot Clint Rhodes in the back the day I left here. Somethin' had to give."

"Rhodes?"

"Yeah. Clint. A blamed good waddie. Ain't many like him."

Clay gathered the reins in his hand. "I'm goin' up home now. If there's any settlin' to be done you know where you can find me. I'm thinkin' you'll want me for trial on that gunhand I killed before I left. I'll stand it if you want me to. I was in the right."

Jack Harris tugged at his hat brim and rubbed his mouth with the back of his hand. "Ain't everybody around here hates you, Clay. Most were just mixed up, that's all. Scared, like. There's them that knows you was shootin' in self-defense. They'll speak for you. I will, hang it."

Clay felt a good feeling coming into him. It was like the sun showing again after a night of storm. "Thanks, Jack," he said. "Maybe we ought to have that trial just the same. The law's got to start in somewhere. Can't have a good place to live 'less it's all legal-like."

Old Man Medford stepped out from the gallery and put his hand on Clay's bridle. "Clay," he said. "Dodge Liston's out to your place. Dodge and Sam Chandler. Dodge didn't figure on your comin' back and he was countin' to hold it for his own until it went up for taxes, and then he was goin' to pick it up cheap."

Clay looked down the street. The rain had laid the dust, but it was picking up again. The road was filling with horses, rigs and people. "Dodge, huh. Well, I'll see about Dodge. And Sam, too."

"You be careful of them two," Old Man Medford said. "We got Sam up here to help out with the law and such, but he's lately taken a shine to Dodge's business. Be careful, Clay."

"Yeah, I will," Clay said. He walked the Morgan up the street a few paces, then turned his body in the saddle. "If any of you fellers want to come out and set some time, you're welcome," he said. "And bring your missus. We got a good view out there."

They left Lupe coming at a slow pace and rode hard. The land had a lift in it going upward from the valley and Clay could see the cottonwoods sitting high up there before they'd gotten far out of town. He was coming home again and he felt that he would never get there. He'd never been so impatient about a thing in his life and he knew that Efigio, and even the Morgan, had it, too. They were coming home and they hadn't very far to go.

They saw Sam Chandler lounging at the entrance to the cottonwood lane. His horse was grazing a little way off and he was sitting on a big rock as though Dodge had maybe stationed him out there as a guard, like. He was taking his pleasure and smoking a cigarette and watching them coming in a lazy kind of way; like there was nothing in the world that could ever ruffle him.

They were a hundred yards off when Sam Chandler got a little nervous. They hadn't slowed down like Chandler maybe thought they ought to, out of deference to him, and Clay knew it was getting into him. Clay didn't think that Chandler recognized them yet, but he was getting excited just the same. He stood up from the rock, squashed the cigarette, and shaded his eyes at them. Then, he turned and ran for the rifle sticking from his saddle scabbard.

His arm hurt like the devil but Clay shook a small loop into his reata anyway. He knew what he was going to do with Chandler, now. He'd been mixed up in his head about that man, but he knew what he was going to do now. Fellers like him had to have a lesson coming to them sometime; they had to lose their swagger.

Chandler nearly got them with the rifle. He jerked the thing out and swerved around just as Clay swung the loop at him. He could see Chandler's face and the quick fear coming into it as he recognized the people bearing down upon him. Then the loop settled down around his knees and Clay dogged the end around the saddle pommel. He let the Morgan run the slack out and Chandler made a handsome flip in the air and landed on his back. Clay removed his end from the horn and tossed it to Efigio, who caught it as he swung down to the ground.

Clay kept on going up the lane, hearing the Mexican's laughter at his back.

There was a bend in the alley and Clay turned off into the brush before he came to it. Off in there, he dismounted and pulled his rifle out. He knew Dodge had likely been aware of the disturbance out in front and he had to be more careful now. He had a special kind of treatment in his mind for Dodge and he didn't want anything to spoil it.

He went through the brush quick and quiet. He kept down low and ran in short spurts from one clump of cover to the next. When he came around to the side of the main house he backed off a ways and worked up a slight rise in the ground and hunkered down behind a low rock outcrop. From that place he could see through the side windows. He could see the whole inside front of the house. He could see

Dodge squatting down behind a front window, with his pistol out, looking up the cottonwood lane.

Dodge was less than fifty yards away, his back nearly toward Clay, and he fit into the sights of the Winchester just fine. Clay moved them up and down his body, looking for a good spot. Dodge was so fat and round that he couldn't hardly miss, but he knew it would have to be the best shooting that he'd ever done.

It made him wish he had Pa's old Ballard out there with him. You couldn't hardly beat a Winchester, but he wished he had the Ballard just the same. Hardin had taught him mark-shooting with that gun and there was no make could beat it for a thing like this.

He kept looking for a good place. The sun coming into that room shone on every part of Dodge and he could have his choice. Dodge was wearing light pants, which made it bigger.

Clay scrunched lower on the ground. He got his elbows in solid and felt the stock press smooth and warm against his cheek. He put a slow pressure on the trigger, and increased it. He pulled the trigger right on through the crack of sound.

Dodge jumped. Dodge Liston jumped like some kind of cat. He jumped straight up in the air and he went through the front window all in one motion, and he lit running, with his fat knees pumping high and both hands clamped to his wide bottom. Clay could just see the fine crease the slug had made back there; just see where the pants were burned in a long, straight line. Then Dodge was in the dooryard moving out. He didn't even stop to get his horse, but kept on running. He raised a small spine of dust all the way up to the bend and out of sight.

Clay came down slowly into the dooryard and stood in the sun. He didn't want to go inside just yet. He simply wanted to stand there and get the feel of everything again. He wanted to breathe it into him and get accustomed to knowing it was permanent. No more leaving this place now. No more riding night trails in the Lincoln country. No more anything like that.

He sat down on the gallery floor and gazed up the lane. When Efigio got through lashing Chandler to his horse and sending it back to town he and Lupe would be coming in. They'd get the cooking fire going and they'd have a big feed. By golly, he was surely hungry, now. That'd please Lupe, all right. That'd please her more than anything. Except maybe knowing that nothing would ever bother them again.

He lay back on the floor and cupped his hands behind his head. There was just a faint throbbing in his shoulder now—a clean wound, thank the good Lord. The sun was warm upon him and he could see the cottonwood crowns dust their color against the sky in gentle strokes. A pretty good place for a man to age in, this place was. Feller could look all his life and never find a better.